HOW DO YOU FINISH SOMETHING YOU NEVER KNEW YOU STARTED?

I started writing these words as a way to deal.

An honest stream of consciousness became a true story of inner turbulence. From youthful optimism to cynical truths to utter despair - and maybe even a source of strength.

But I betrayed the words, locking them away so I would not take those thoughts out into the world with me.

These pages have been stuck in a box, without light or air, for almost 20 years.

Coming to terms with our own journey is different for everyone. The secrets we guard the closest are our own true feelings.

But words are meant to breathe, and every story is meant to be told.

THE WALK
A JOURNAL

First published 2022 by Elus Ives

elusivesauthor@gmail.com
www.elusivesauthor.com

ISBN 978-0-6455640-2-0

Cover by Elus Ives

THE WALK

A JOURNAL

by Elus Ives

for those who feel they don't belong where they are

prologue:
to build your wings, first jump off a cliff

the house teetered on the edge of the world, threatening to slip at any moment. A little green lizard with the eyes of a pet and a predator climbed into it and tried to pull it back to safety, but it was no use. The house rocked there, neither hopeful nor tragic... hesitating somewhere between finding a way to show it was alive, or just going ahead and being dead.

the bright orange sky above was the symbol of all the things that had not gone before, and smiled down on the scene with loathing and amusement, listening as the tune played.

all the screams had a meaning, but none of them knew each other, so they fought and fought and fought some more, not knowing that they were brothers. I couldn't tell what they were trying to say, but I couldn't stop laughing so I don't think I would have been able to understand them anyway.

an old man walked into the picture, with flowers under his arm and said they were supposed to be in his hair but he couldn't find his head, and I said I understood.

even though the rain was threatening to search for us, the benevolent clouds promised not to let it find us, at least not this century, and the cars were pleased.

below us the sea was vast and infinite; a deep, dark blue so clear that I could see right into it and the whales looked up and winked at me with an understanding as infinite as their home. The water was perfectly still, maddeningly calm as far

1

as I could see and I wanted to hurl everything in sight into it, break that pure surface, again and again. The blue pulled my eyes into it, bottomless and seductive, so that I thought I could breathe in there, as if it were sweet air with a liquid caress. But I knew better.

the house was almost over the edge, for all its procrastinating, and the lizard gave up when it realised that the house wanted to fall. As the lizard let go, the house wanted to stay, but it still went over. The dogs began to howl and the wind began to howl and for a moment the old man began to howl but when I bumped into him he went off the cliff and that shut him up. I was instantly ashamed because the flowers were weeping, and I saw that he was supposed to be howling, but also that he was better off dead, so one by one, I threw them into the house. It wasn't easy at first but then I found my rhythm, and they just sailed in and I knew that it was the way it was supposed to be. The house was floating on the water, a prone body slowly breaking up on the surface. The water was perfectly flat again, as if I could walk upon it, over to the house, and I was angry because I hadn't seen the ripples when the house was falling in, and now my chance had passed.

the green lizard had slunk off somewhere, guilty at killing the house, and a multicoloured plane flew into the world from somewhere. It swooped down as if to pick us up but just scooped up the cliff and all the cars so that there wasn't much space left for anyone except the guitarist who seemed to survive anything. I shouted at the plane to pick up the body of the old man, but it just went whining by, up into the sky above us, where it circled like a great carrion bird with one eye on the corpse of the house. The old man rose from the water, mumbling epithets at the bird but not at me, and disappeared into a cloud only to come floating out on the air currents with his new wings flapping, passing continually, endlessly over the *house, looking for his flowers, but not bothering to look for his head.*

the guitarist finally began to play and it was the most beautiful sound I had ever heard, so beautiful that all around us the world began to explode into the most vibrant colours ever invented, plus a few that were new and shone proudly as if they were thinking thoughts of their own brilliance. I looked perfection in the face for a quarter of a second but then the singer came to see the colours and sang to them so that the singer and the guitarist were competing and all the colours doubled up in agony, and died a death just as ugly as their short life had been beautiful.

i didn't want to know that this was the way it was supposed to be, so I began to cry. The dogs didn't howl though, they just wept with great reverence and respect. Suddenly I began to laugh again, filling myself with such hysteria that the clouds moved away from us and the singer was afraid. The violence of my laughter attracted a dozen more planes, but they didn't come to me, they just circled us and each other with an order that looked like confusion.

the rain began to fall all around but the clouds kept their promise and none fell on us in our little kingdom, and both the singer and the guitarist were filled with pride, each thinking it was in appreciation for their song. I walked to the wall of raindrops. I put my tongue to the drops to taste the sweetest nectar ever created and I wanted some more, more than I had wanted anything in my life, but the clouds stopped raining and wouldn't let me have any. In anger I stalked off to the furthest dry rock and sat down to sulk, to find that I had crushed the green lizard, and it thanked me before it died like the house. But I could not appreciate its gratitude because I was still yearning for the water.

a deep sadness filled me, but as I looked around at the cliff, at the perfect ocean and the orange sky, at the still living and the newly dead, the great sadness turned into an even greater, more filling understanding.

suddenly all was all right with the world and I felt hope and lightness in my existence. I realised the openness of this incomprehension, that nothing is set.

i was free to walk away from the rock, and I did so. I was free to walk to the cliff edge and look down, and I did that too. I was free to throw myself into nothingness and feel the warm air rush up past me, and I jumped. I was free...

(19.12.96)

ONE

GET UP. START WALKING.

1.

first term, final year

and here he was, with his wings not yet built, and his mind in the air where they were destined to fly, and he looked at the world with a clearer understanding. And then immediately a greater confusion where that destiny was kept at bay by his life, and this conflict had a mind of its own. Predictably, he was excluded, with nothing but the music in his head and the notes just beyond his memory, so that he had many to look forward to, but none to look back on.

he drew himself out of the ocean in this place where youth comes to meet life, and doubted that he would ever really see the others again, even if he met them on the road that led up the beach into the forest. It was the only path to follow, and he entered the beauty with great fear as his feet passed over the beach, collecting no sand but leaving footprints as indelible as if they were carved in stone, and just as cold. As he entered the forest it took the appearance of a great wasteland in his mind, one that felt as barren as cold white moons but he could not see the true infinity amongst these trees.

silence reigned as he looked around, wondering what he would meet. The path disappeared in front of him, and he turned around, expecting to see it disappear behind, but it was so noticeably there, beckoning him with warmth and promise.

But he knew that beyond it was the same beach he'd come from, and he didn't have enough time to make that mistake.

he walked on, driving the fear from himself, and making friends with his confusion, and wishing for rain that would never taste the same again.

(12.02.97)

2.

born to a road in a forest, the walker

he walked and walked and walked. The sun shone down and he walked. The wind rushed at him from every conceivable direction, threatening to throw him aside, and he walked. The inevitable rain pelted him like pebbles flung by a childish god, and he walked.

it was his nature, to walk. He seemed incapable of running, perhaps because he chose not to, but probably because he had never learned how. He just continued with that same pace, consistent, which would never tire him but would eat up the leagues without his noticing. And he knew better than to look back. To do that would be to re-enter another world, one that he had left the day he realised that his path was different. That it was in another direction, that it was never-ending. Maybe he was meant to walk the earth. So life is meant to be a journey, not a destination... but what is a journey really worth without a place at the end of it, where he could stop, and find himself in a place, *the* place? Where he would know, really know where he was, who he was, what he was, and be satisfied with all of them.

but maybe he knew just enough for the time being. Like a refugee who makes his life in a new place, surrounded by strange things and people he had never known, but still connected to some deeper, hardwired knowledge of his own identity... he could look, and see, and learn, but never lose sight of himself, the self that felt right.

or maybe the self that felt least wrong. Perhaps the two weren't so different? But he felt that there must be some distinction and perhaps that was the journey, to find the one that was real. To travel in any direction, and always be on the same road, walking to the same destination.

that left only the question of the destination's existence, and the journey to take him there. He could live with that.

X

3.

after a few weeks of this eternity he realised that he should not have entered the forest. He wasn't ready. It was a mistake. But it was too late because the time was lost and he'd never be able to find it again, and searching would only eat away valuable minutes he didn't have.

...suddenly the forest became denser and denser around him and he had an epiphany.

he shouldn't have been unprepared to enter the forest, because part of him was always there; because his mind lived in it and it lived in his mind, with the rest of his life peering in trying to get a look. He began to feel more at home when the great black bird that ate the crow came swooping down to obliterate all sight of the dark green canopy with it's flapping, pounding wings.

he laughed. It looked him in the eye, recognised him without acknowledging his existence, before breaking up through the canopy and showering him with leaves like green rain. He picked up a leaf and tasted it for sweetness, but it was bitter, very bitter for something so familiar. He concluded that it must be good for him and gorged himself on bitterness until it turned to dark blood in his veins and a darker song in his head, and he continued to walk.

(19.03.97)

4.

...it had been a strange day. The planet was too slow so he imagined the trees crashing violently to a pensive earth that was both mother and slave and took each fall like the stroke of a whip, with tenderness and resentment. He knew that this was his crime, to destroy what existed with a wrecking ball that shouted its purpose in a silent way that ate into his hatred and fed his confusion, but he didn't care, because it had been a good day otherwise. But it was overflowing with unreal promises of goodness and complications of logic, and he wasn't sure which he wanted. So he walked, and he saw. But it was the way he saw that surprised him.

(21.03.97)

5.

unrequited pt. 1

the blue in her eyes mingled with the salt in his soul and he knew she wasn't the one.

for her quietly forlorn eyes were far, far deeper than the hole in his heart and to fall in would be the only mortal decision he could make. And he knew his immortality would keep him from drinking her blue but also from drowning. Then the confusion took over and the red in his head was better than it had ever been, except for the time he awoke from yesterday's reality and fell to the earth in a shower of dreams, each one a window to the diversity of the surface of the world, but only a few to the meaning of the deep.

so into his confusion he withdrew, but took a little of her spirit in his pocket, so that his loneliness would be a sight for her to look on without seeing for the rest of his journey. And he looked back many times because he knew it was safe and she would not be there, mocking and contemptuous like everyone else.

and then, inevitably, the sky greyed and blackened and turned, and he wondered if he had made a mistake.

(30.03.97)

6.

the space between our faculties

the ground was warm, as if heated by all the goodness and love of a sun that would never understand it. He walked slowly, allowing each step to caress the earth that was not quite his home. A white bird flew across his path and he greeted it cordially, but it sailed past much too fast and did not even notice him. *Alas,* he thought, *a meeting not meant to be.* A black bird flapped noisily past too, and again their eyes met and he looked down into his own mind. He stopped for a second and watched the dark figure float in the sky, becoming smaller and smaller until it blotted out the sun. And he felt cold again and pulled his being closer around him, and waited until all the clouds passed and the warmth fell onto his face once more. He smiled wryly, already reliving the passing of the dark bird, said *yes, yes* to himself, and understood.

so he made a small decision to keep from having to make any others, and walked with his eyes upon his shoes where they would not get lost.

this is good, he thought, and the faces nodded approvingly looking the other way. He sat in a place where the world was green and let the sweet smells of the earth float through him like huge flocks of small birds for whom direction was no matter. And the sky was blue but not so blue, not yet, and the orange hid for a while but he waited patiently for its return because he knew it would not be pleased if he went on without it. But it only streaked through the sky for a short, short while, as he contemplated the long, long mile and thought he came across a little sense.

confidence appeared for a millisecond. The eyes could see properly for just this fraction of an eon but that even a tiny piece of time was enough to be real, and even though the chaos thrived he saw a path through it and knew the work could get done. All those fields, and no time to reap what he had not been able to sow, but he knew he would reap. This he had to know.

(26.04.97)

7.

but sometimes what the walker knew was what the walker read and what the walker wrote, and indeed, sometimes the two greyed into each other and became one.

he came to a place where what was written was all around him, and given to him by something old and wise, and he knew this age and wisdom was just a symbol of something older and wiser, so he read the words without question.

'hope sat on a boulder and looked at trust. And after a few seconds they recognised each other, like old friends who had forgotten the faces but suddenly remembered the feelings. But it had been too long since they had danced and their steps were false, and all the embarrassed laughing in the world could not drive away the dark, creeping fear that there wasn't enough time to learn the steps again. Who would teach them? Who could?

'but then they saw another who had long been in absence and whose face had been taken in vain for moons upon moons and they smiled and said hello to faith. But faith was old and weak, separated from heart by oceans and eons, and smiled and said, *I cannot survive much longer, and I am doomed if heart is lost.* So they vowed to find heart and set off through the world.

'they saw many things. First they crossed the desert and found love, naked and alone and afraid, and they asked, *why are you so?*

'and love said, *every day I feel the warmth of the sun and begin to grow and find myself, but the day darkens and the moon comes. And it makes me shiver and tremble with fear because its cold is so sharp. And then the sun returns for a while, and then the moon. Again and again. And I ask them, why can I not just be, why do you make me grow and shrink, make me so fickle? But they do not answer.*

'so hope and trust carried love from the desert, though the exertion made trust tired and questioning.

'then they came to the mountain and climbed slowly, hoping that heart had found the summit. But they only found vanity - because vanity had been the only one with the desire to climb to the top and live there.

'they asked if vanity had seen heart but vanity just laughed and said contemptuously, *only I have the power to climb the mountain, and as I look down upon the world, I survey my kingdom. I do not have time to look for your friend, my perfection is all that matters.*

'and love said, *that cannot be true, two with a burden have also climbed this mountain.*

'and there was uncertainty in the beautiful eyes of vanity. But hope was affected by this meeting and felt both flawed and dirtied.

'next they arrived at the edge of the ocean and found

friendship swimming through the dark waters. Friendship was tired, swimming with greater difficulty in each stroke.

'they asked, *what is wrong in the ocean of friendship?*

'and friendship replied, *the waters grow and grow and grow and I am too weak to swim between all the shores. Some places I must forsake in order to reach others and they do not all believe in me. Hope and trust and love are lost, and I meet fear and loneliness every day, laughing, madness in their eyes, drunk with success.*

'and friendship was told, *we are hope and trust and love. And we are tired, as you are. But heart must be found, or faith will die and be gone forever.*

'so friendship carried them across the ocean to the shore where the forest grew, without a word of pain. And as they entered the forest, friendship, weakened beyond measure, slipped deeper into the dark blue waters and continued to swim slowly, inches away from sinking and leagues away from rest, and destined never to reach certain shores.

'and in the forest, it was dark and forbidding and every step was another danger. They lost their way and saw many strange and terrible things and were afraid. Then they met cynicism and cynicism's eyes were pure anguish.

'and they asked, *where is heart?* for they could summon no other words.

'but cynicism said, *if you don't know, then there is no point in telling you.*

'so they left the chaos of the forest where cynicism lived and continued to search, but did not find heart. When they returned to the place they had left, faith was dying.

'they said, *we do not have the strength to continue, we have failed you, and heart is lost.*

'and faith smiled with gratitude and said, *at least you tried, and love was rescued.*

'suddenly the skies darkened and cold winds blew and fearfully they wondered why. Behind them, cynicism walked in from the world. Hope was trembling with fear, trust seething with anger and love shrinking from the cold.

'but faith smiled and whispered, *heart. You came back.*

'and cynicism knelt at faith's deathbed, eyes filled with tears that would not fall, and said, *I'm sorry, I tried, but the world was too strong and I was defeated.*

'faith only smiled again and said sadly, *some must fall into despair, so that others can know what joy is worth.*

'wordlessly, cynicism took faith's hand and filled the dying one with strength until cynicism's own was exhausted, and the dark one lay back upon the rocks and looked up at the blue sky. For a second it was the most beautiful thing in the world, and then the eyes of the dark one closed, and never opened again.

'faith rose, saved but weak still, and said, *I go to look for heart, who lives again somewhere in the world.*

'the others asked, *how can you know this?*

'and faith looked down at the body of the dark fallen one and did not smile, and replied, *all things are measured by the measures of other things, and heart will survive, just as cynicism lives on in the strong, and the broken.'*

and the walker looked up to find truth in the eyes of the one who had tried to teach him, but there was no one else in the forest.

(26.04.97)

18

alone, with others

the walker came to a place where nothing made sense and could have called it home. The walls around the forest town went high above and deep below, and within that ring, insanity thrived. A woman with the eye of an angry dog lured him into the bar but all the horses were talking excitedly as if night was coming and he was afraid. But the sign was bright, and although it said something he could not comprehend, its glow seemed to have more to do with the day than the night.

he didn't need a drink. So he sat down on the stairs and looked at the people inside and silence filled them as they stared at the newcomer, unashamedly, as if enthralled by this thing only because it was new. All their eyes were blank and empty and no wheels turned within them. The man at the nearest table looked as if someone had stolen half of his brain and hidden it in his glass, leaving the half that contained only the ability to keep looking for it.

somehow the walker knew that the people would never turn to their lives but stare at him forever, so he left. At the door he turned back and saw a room of people staring at an empty staircase and pity was born in his soul.

outside the dog-eyed woman was raving at the coming of the hound and a hound walked past but she didn't notice. The horses were laughing because a star had appeared in the sky. Night fell, crashing on the town with a vengeance so complete that it deafened the horses and they stood still, looking at each other in awe. The walker sat down on the step and watched a woman cross the street as, one by one, the stars began to fall to the lampposts and electricity was born. She was tall and faceless but there was movement in her eyes and he felt ashamed that all he could see were the shiny buckles on her shoes. But they winked at him until she had passed, and he forgot what she looked like. He looked over to the horses but they were cars now, with brighter eyes and shinier coats, but they were still creatures that carried other creatures and he realised that they had not evolved at all.

he walked across the street into the hotel and paid for a room with smiles and promises, but when he got there the smiles and promises were in someone else's room. His room was padded from floor to ceiling and the door did a clever trick and disappeared when he closed it, and all he had for company were the dirty footprints that didn't quite fit his feet. So he ran into the wall a few hundred times until he couldn't feel his face, but that was all right because he'd never had much use for it anyway.

then he stood in the centre and spun around and around and around until he remembered to stop and the room didn't. He had to sit down to keep from staying on his feet and when he did the door reappeared, spinning around him so fast that the whole room was an open door and he just got up and walked out.

outside the world was filled with symbols of lies and violence and fireworks raged in his head until someone threw a bucket of water in his face. At first he thought that the bucket had broken his nose and he realised that the feeling in his face was coming back, but when he felt it, it seemed like the face of someone else. The bright lights were blinding and beautiful and he realised he was looking into the eyes of the faceless woman and he looked for her buckles eagerly but she'd changed her shoes and all the wondrous lights in the universe could never undo that injustice.

he decided that now was the time to leave the town, there wasn't enough madness here, and he walked along the high, deep wall, looking for the exit. He came to an enormous sign that said EXIT but there was no gap, only a freshly dug grave with two geriatrics and a beluga whale fighting for it. So he continued along the wall until he came to the entrance and said he wanted his money back but was told that he had learned something.

and he wondered if that was true and wandered away, back the way he had come.

(29.04.97)

9.

conversations with the devil (one)

the world began to spin and spin and all of a sudden he didn't know where he was. A cold grey light settled in his mind and offered no comfort, because everything it shone upon taught him another way to look down at the ground and keep walking. A smart blue wind blew in from the south, too clever and strong to walk against, keeping him where he was, so he decided to sit down, away for a while, and try not to think.

a plane passed overhead, dropping sound like the only bird in the sky and the way it moved looked mindless, like a terrified animal crashing through the forest undergrowth running forever into the waiting trap. He watched until it was a speck in the sky and then just a figment of his imagination, and wondered how many individual worlds could sit in the space between a finger and a speck. A rainbow appeared in the forgiving sky, though all the world was as dry as the last glass and just as transparent, and he realised with a shiver that all the sky was the rainbow and all its colours were blue. But not *the* blue, just a cheap imitation with no guarantee.

but that thought was harsh and he felt ashamed because unlike words, your thoughts can't be unthought and some things you can't take back.

so he tried to be a better person and looked down at the only things that he really knew and asked his shoes to carry him.

but they pointed in two different directions and he laughed at the predictability of it all, and they only smiled up at him sheepishly, apologetic.

he looked up at the trees and thought he saw the devil dancing with abandon from treetop to treetop, and he spoke,

- *why do you do this to me?*

the devil stopped, shocked that the mortal could see, and its eyes said everything. And the walker was filled with great dread, not because the devil was real, but because the devil was weak and pathetic and stupid, and wasn't doing this at all.

for a second they looked deep into each other's eyes and the devil said,

- *you're not like the others... what are you?*

and the sky stopped being blue, and the trees were still and silent, and the shoes smiled no more, because the walker looked inside the devil and spoke a terrible truth when he asked in that quiet voice that was almost never heard,

- why do you fear me, when I fear myself?

(19.05.97)

10.

conversations with the devil (two)

the cold wind blew over his soul and the confusion came searching. But somehow, the confusion he knew began to become sense, a creeping rationality that could not be ignored. Every thought led back to the same place, that cool field, the green where the madness was kept at bay, those howling wolves were out of reach, even though they threatened to leap into the world, snapping and snarling and ecstatic. He knew they would catch him if he ran, but this didn't feel like running, it felt more like stopping and resting on the grass, and finding another direction in which to walk.

he knew that everything around him was a question that summoned the answer to everything, and that answer was again the *best possible* option, a purely rational animal that seemed so logical but somehow always grew into more winding, beautiful chaos. Inside, he knew he was tied to constantly finding that best answer: the best he could do under the circumstances, the best the universe would allow him, the best that he could be. The best possible solution that never worked.

he felt the presence in the air again, and realised that

the cold wind was his first warning and he should have heeded it. He looked up at the treetops and saw the figure crouching on the highest leaf. The clouds began to darken, preventing the sun from having to look on the arrival.

- *welcome back,* said the chill voice of the devil.

- *i have seen the weakness of your nature,* said the walker, and knew instantly that he had made a mistake.

the devil began to laugh in its high-pitched, painful tone, and began to fidget upon the tree, its glee rising. It was the deviant creature, the frozen emotion that always came back to haunt you, the cold smile that always found its way to your lips. And the walker saw that this being was entirely its own reality, not a figment or a ghost story or a convenient construct from a fairy tale for believers. And that whatever the devil was, it really came from a frozen wasteland, a far worse place than he had ever imagined.

- *and I have seen yours,* said the devil, unable to contain its pleasure.

the walker kept silent, desperately trying not to commit another error. He didn't know if he had witlessly started a battle of wits, where his opponent was the only one with combat experience.

- *how are your dreams?* asked the devil, knowing the answer full well. *Having trouble remembering? Too bad, they make such interesting viewing. All those colours, and so many emotions! I do envy you,*

- *yes, I know,* said the walker, interrupting without thinking.

the devil stopped, and the walker could see that a nerve had been exposed.

- *do you really? guessing the thoughts of another is*

24

such an interesting mortal phenomenon, it's almost -

- *charming,* said the walker.

again that look of uncertainty flashed in the devil's eyes, for the briefest of moments.

- *that's not really the word I would have used,* stammered the devil, *I would rather have said -*

- *pitiful,* supplied the walker.

there was a look of pain in the hellish creature, and it began to look around furtively, as if for some kind of help from the trees, but they were looking the other way.

- *your eyes, they have the confusion within them, I can see,* began the devil, *but you'll never get rid of the chaos you feel because -*

- *because it lives here, where it knows it has a home,* said the walker, quickly and quietly, almost masterful.

there was a yelp of pain from the devil and the wind whipped up around the walker. The trees began to sway and the clouds moved to and fro in fear. The devil began to mumble and mutter under its breath, and fidgeted, this time with panic. It flew from treetop to treetop, but not like the first time, now trying to find a haven as the walker began to shout, anything and everything, hysteria in his voice. He sounded as if he were trying to kill the devil with screams, or else trying to exorcise something from his own mind with verbal torture.

there was a cry from the devil, and it disappeared into the sky like it was diving into an ocean, and the walker was thrown back violently to the ground.

when he awoke, all was calm and peaceful, but he was alone again.

(02.06.97)

11.

conversations with the devil (three)

the walker could see nothing in front of him, only look back at his meetings with the devil. He wondered if he had won the game, or only scored a point, but just wondering that was enough to scare any other focus from his mind. So he sat in the sun where it was safe and where no thought was of any consequence, as if he had come to the last day of the world and it meant nothing to his soul.

he sat on the bench in the green place, looking over the sky and feeling the warmth wash the numbness from his fingers. He closed his eyes to feel the sun more keenly, but a cold shiver ran down the length of his body, like he had been wrapped from head to toe in cold plastic, a shroud from the morgue where all excitement now resided.

When he opened his eyes the sun was full upon his face, but still he shivered. He was no longer alone on the bench. He squinted at the figure now seated beside him, and was afraid.

- *two sceptics on a park bench trying to feel a useless sun...* said that quiet, cold voice.

the walker moved to the end of the bench, and wondered how the devil could exist so openly under the burning star, and realised that the devil was as adaptable as he was. He said nothing; being this close to the creature had driven the speech from him. The devil looked at him in the eye, and he turned away quickly. The devil in turn looked at the sun.

- *i know, the walker,* said the devil, haltingly, as if each word was coming to it like a slow art. *The walker, walks, to me. In truth, he fears, this, chaos. So. I come to him, to show him, the way. But. He spurns me. He does not accept, my generosity. ...Why?*

the walker did not answer. He wanted to jump up and run, flee madly into the sun but his feet were lead, and he was now too cold to move. That voice crept into the furthest reaches of his brain, insistent, hastening.

- i came, to the world. I searched, for the one that needed to be found. I allowed myself to be recognised -

- you did not allow it, stammered the walker. But the rest of the accusation died in his heart.

- i did! I let you see the world as it is, not as they tell you it is! the devil spat quickly in that high, cold voice.

the walker summoned all his courage and spoke, though fearfully.

- you're lying... you were surprised. You asked me what I was. You did not know me.

- i know you! cried the devil in that mad, cold voice, fidgeting upon the bench. *I have watched you, watched your life! I have seen you walk fitfully upon the surface of the world, grow into the one that you are.*

- what is that? asked the walker, falling into the trap.

- you are the dark side of the moon. You are the one that sees when the world falls into turmoil. You are the one who walks through the disaster, before, during, and after. You are the walker.

- i do not know this, said the walker painfully, tears in his eyes.

- you know! cried the devil, and the walker feared the

creature would reach out and grasp him. *You know it every time you open your eyes! Every step that you take tells you! You do not belong here!*

The devil leaned over and screamed into the walker's ear, its cold, stinking breath obliterating the wind, its voice piercing the walker's mind.

- you are the walker! You are me! You are mine!

the walker was overcome and leapt from the bench, running from the devil who sat laughing insanely behind him. He ran faster than he had ever done, his heart bursting from his body, his eyes shut against the sun that had betrayed him, and his soul in a place he could not find.

(08.06.97)

12.

conversations with the devil (four)

the next meeting between the walker and the devil was inevitable, and inevitably it was violent.

they did not speak but their communication could not be clearer. The walker found himself racked with fever and writhed upon the ground like a snake somehow under the influence of its own venom, lashing out at everything within reach, and hating with a sadness he alone could understand. And the world came to him all the while, pouring itself like molten lead upon him, threatening to fix him with a burden, a shroud, a coffin, forever. And he screamed silently; no one could hear him but the creature from nowhere and everywhere, who sat amongst the leaves of the nearest tree and grinned maniacally.

the walker stood, and summoned all the strength he could, and rushed at the devil, his heart filled with anger. But the devil was light-footed and danced around him, spinning with glee like a child before the burden of reason. The shoes of the walker were confused, all they wanted was to walk through the forest, but their master, their slave, was without direction. The devil began to laugh as the walker fell again, laughing so loud that the leaves turned away from the torture. It ripped a branch from a tree and began to beat the walker with it, sadistic, ecstatic. It gave another branch to the walker, offering a fight, but the walker had no strength and could not lift the branch or himself. So the devil began to kick the walker, humiliation its intent, and the walker could do nothing in defence. But then the sky came to the aid of the walker, turning that familiar shade of orange, and a cloud passed over the pair, showering them with a cool, sweet rain. The devil hid under a tree and watched the rain wash the fever from the body of the kneeling figure. Then the walker slowly raised his head and looked into the eyes of the creature, and the devil saw for a second something worse than any devil or any hell, and knew that this had gone too far. So it fled the forest, diving into the sky again, disappearing like an arrow into the air, and the rain ceased to fall, the sky trying to communicate. But the walker had changed again, and screamed with hurt and rage and sorrow, and all the truces he had ever known were broken.

(21.06.97)

13.

hometown vs. the world

the walker stayed on the road for many days, feeding on the sounds that kept the sanity at bay. He walked with purpose, but he knew it was born from the place where the devil had tried to best him, and from a blind determination to stay on the road, no matter what. He knew that this clarity of thought was not going to last, that his pace would slow, and he would look around at the chaos of the forest that pushed itself into this road not taken, under a sky that refused to be blue.

but he tried not to think about the sky, it was still too full of the promise of things that had not happened simply because he had tried to wish them into being. He looked down instead.

he came one evening to a river, black and swift and dead, and knew that he must cross. Predictably there was a bridge, and he thought, *another*, with sadness. For this bridge was also change, the brother of the change that found its way into his soul, when the devil had finally reached out and touched him. And it looked like all the other bridges that had come before, that he had rushed across, blindly, desperately. It beckoned silently, but he could feel the emptiness of the road beyond even more than that of the one behind, sensing it more than he could see it. Somehow that emptiness was seductive and he was attracted so strongly that he found himself at the end of the road and the beginning of the change, through no will of his own. He looked at his shoes but they slept like they were drunk with walking and no longer of any use but the next day, and he knew he had been forced to make this decision alone.

he sat for a while, cross-legged at the threshold, while the silence found him like arrows from unseen foes, and the bridge was patient. He thought, *that road is the same as this, I know it already. There is no one on it.*

so he decided that he was wasting time he didn't have, and placed one foot onto the bridge to make the crossing. Suddenly a dark bird swooped down on a dark wind from nowhere and fell like a stone straight onto the middle of the bridge, and lay there, a heap of wings and feathers and black, and he was filled with fear. He could see the clouds rolling in from the south and the bird refused to move and he knew it was dead. But in that same thought he had another: he knew what to do. He stepped from the bridge and looked at his feet. Between them lay a match, the most beautiful, most violent invention. He lit it, and placed it on the footprint he had left on the bridge, and together they began to burn. Soon the entire structure was a writhing joyous conflagration that screamed into the deepening night. He walked slowly away along the bank, looking for another road but now the forest was very, very close. He heard a cry and turned to see the bird rising in the sky, flames with wings into the stars. He turned, the cold biting at his eyes, and walked with that same blind determination. But in his heart he knew two things. The first was that all the truces were still broken. The second was that he would meet the same bridge again, with a greater temptation to cross.

and of course he thought to himself, *I'll burn that bridge when I come to it.*

(24.06.97)

14.

outside, inside your head

he did not know what drove him more; the dark, silent chaos that lived in his mind or his soul's need to see the sun. At times he thought they were the same thing, but other times he had the feeling they were in conflict, each striving for dominance.

conflict. Yes, that was the word. Nothing blended into anything else; always there was an abrupt ending and a new beginning exploding with life. Yet surely everything was connected, each thread interwoven with the next, like the roots under the surface of a grassy field. It gave the illusion of logic, of coherence. But every so often the grasses would stir, be led by the wind this way and that, and the roots would struggle to hold together. He wondered if the weaver in this case was in the throes of some delirious insanity. But he held on with an unreasoning determination; or perhaps it was just the strengthless lack of will that is the staying power of the weak.

every day was a clutter of thoughts and emotions, as if the light he steered by flitted around in his brain, an intoxicated butterfly over the grasses of mind and body and soul. No thought lasted more than a fraction of a second, no thought at the end of a second seemed related to the one at the start. No emotions seemed real and he wished they were something he could see so that he could count them and know some measure of comprehension or control. But the only reality was a bright burning sun in this place of flawless blue skies and he hadn't seen that for a long while. The shoes on his feet were meant for the desert, this he knew. But it was far away, so far that he couldn't even see it in his future, only feel it in the breezes that touched his face and drove away the cold. Too far to exist in this world, only the next. The past was gone, and here he was.

he imagined himself in that world of beautiful simplicity. Yellow sun. Blue sky. White sand. The complications of the forest lived in another place. He turned, and turned, and saw only the horizon. No mountains to threaten their power, no trees to whisper their inconsistencies.

suddenly trees began to spring from the ground, growing from nothing, fed by nothing, eating up the earth. Green blocked the sky and fought with the blue and the sun became gentler but the winds began to cool. Flocks of birds filled the heavens in formations that crisscrossed every inch of the sky but they were warplanes, the birds of conflict, and the drone of their engines was deafening.

he shielded his eyes from a shocked orange sun and watched as the undercarriages opened, a synchronised disembowelling, and black birds rained from the sky, swooping down over the trees, their wings flapping with a confusion that looked like order. In their beaks each held a scrap of paper, a message, an epiphany. With great cries of freedom they dropped them upon the forest in great cooling showers of knowledge, of the greatest treasure known to humankind, of answers. As soon as they released one, they regurgitated another that appeared in their beaks to be dropped, and on and on they gave up what was inside them. In a second he understood. The birds were his thoughts, the messages his feelings. He ran joyously to receive them, gathered them into his arms like children, as more and more rained upon him. He took the first with the realisation that the wait was finally over.

but they were in a language he could not understand,

gifts from a world that could not understand him.

despairingly he looked up. There were more.

they were countless.

(16.07.97)

15.

the sky's so blue it hurts my eyes

he returned to the cliff with the intention of walking off it into the nothingness that encompassed his soul.

Any life that grew within him was away today and even all the things he thought were *right* had become *maybes* that didn't know where they were going. He said hello to the blue sky and saw that the ocean was moving, ever so slowly as if there was an enormous creature stirring sensually beneath the surface. He looked over the edge and saw only the colours of the creature but not its shape, and the colours were so beautiful that he thought he was in the wrong place. He looked around but saw all the frightening things he had come to know, and knew this danger was the safety he was used to.

the last day had been the strangest in a while, but he knew that was because he had seen the strangeness for what it was this time, and realised that he was beginning to tell himself the truth, or at least a version of it.

he went to visit the joy that lived in the sunshine, for she was closer here. The only one who still seemed real, despite his deep, unwavering awareness that for him, sometimes the mirage was yet to be found, under the surface not upon it. And when she spoke and he saw joy and despair in the same sunshine this time and allowed himself to be scared by this, he pushed that fear away quietly, efficiently, and the sky agreed to be blue again for a while, in admiration of that other place, the one he'd left so foolishly. And for a second he was not sure if he was pushing her away with it. Or if he was escaping.

he stood alone at the edge for an endless moment, one foot in front of the other, sliding on the sepia glasses he sometimes used to make the bright world into slightly more bearable colours, and called the breeze to his face. It came to him like an excited puppy, nearly knocking him over with its exuberance, and he laughed with the joy and colour that had been missing for a long time. He had placed all his love in the hands of the sky, and all his feelings of betrayal at its feet when it was so grey for so long. But the blue was back and he alone could understand, and he realised that it may be this way for all time.

somehow that didn't seem so bad, so he leapt from the cliff with more strength than he had ever admitted to and sailed through the air for what seemed like a day longer than his existence and exalted in the wonderful violence of it all, this feeling, this day, this life.

when he finally came to rest he was on the deck of the sun boat, clipping through the waters that were the world, and heading for the sun-god that waited so patiently, like a king lion in the grasses, powerful but alone. But he was not ready, and made his apologies to the sun for changing his mind, saying, *you'll have to be alone a little while longer, there's too much to see, too many to be...will you watch for me?*

and the sun replied, *I will.*

but he knew that if he left the realm of the sun his soul would be in jeopardy, more than ever, because it was such a short journey from complete control to complete anarchy when you were the walker. He looked across and saw another boat a short distance away, parallel, in a synchronisation too perfect, and the devil was at the bow, trussed up like the most pathetic bow head ever crafted. The devil turned his head to the walker and its eyes begged for mercy and forgiveness and love, and the walker laughed ruthlessly in tune with the guitars, realising that he had a long way to go before his mind was freed from the darkness.

he stepped off the deck and was engulfed by the water that tasted of no salt. He floated serenely on his back and felt the fish that were sharks sniff at his body, and escort him to the place in which he could not live and was the only home he would ever know. When he arrived at the shore he felt that he should pay the sharks something for their guidance and knew only a piece of his flesh would mean anything to them. He laughed at the sight of the predictability that might become his trademark, and offered them the only organ he had no use for, his heart.

as he walked upon the beach again, he felt the cold sand between his mind and his soul, and was not as afraid as the first time, because he knew that the forest was his, and all within it would live in his life as completely as his own being. He closed his eyes to hear the music more clearly and felt lifted when he found the cacophony within the notes, and spoke to the trees; *I have returned.*

and all the forest turned in fear to greet him, and he saw the beginning within the ending that signalled a new chapter in the life of the walker.

(08.08.97)

36

16.

final year, final term

but some chapters refuse to be closed.

the walker realised he had become complacent when he took his eyes off the ground and walked into the hole that waited, either like a starving demon or a yawning god, he knew not which. He felt himself fall and thought nothing of it, as the cold and hot winds rushed up past, alternating, taking their turns to batter his face. He fell for an eternity, his hands in his pockets with the air of not caring a damn and his shoes resting, but that last should have been his warning, had he listened, and watched, and known. Every so often he collided with something and destroyed it, and was a little destroyed himself, but none of that mattered. Nothing mattered except for a light at the end of the tunnel that shone with the future, but very late he realised he was falling away from it. He could not think whether it was too late, and he realised he could not think at all, and perhaps this was the problem.

so he decided to halt the fall but his power had waned and he clutched ineffectually at the things that swept up away from him, each one turning in the dim light to reveal itself as something of great importance. And as he fell he heard a song about the sun where he was born and the night where he lived and the death of the angels, and he realised he had been hiding from the complications. He passed a dolphin as he swam downward in this delirium but didn't know what it was, except for the clock it held between its teeth that chimed a thirteenth hour for those that were too late, who saw things in a light already used up, already passed on, and somewhere else.

he passed the devil who sat rubbing chafed wrists, but the walker was not seen as he flew past in his tailspin, and remembered that adaptability was their link, and would be again. He crashed through a meteor shower of books he had no time to write, that stared at him with blank pages, empty worlds, and he couldn't hold on to even one. A tear escaped his eye and fell beneath him and he watched it for an eternity of miles as they sailed down together, a drop of life just out of reach of his pleading hand. It grew smaller and smaller and disappeared, and the realisation that his tears had begun to fall faster than he did made him decide that enough was enough, and he stood up. The stop played havoc with his balance and changed his understanding before he had the sense to prevent it. But the deed was done and the walls of the hole turned into the trees of the forest, and he instinctively put one foot in front of the other.

he saw that he wasn't in as much danger as he had thought, if only he relied on what was in his head. So the walk continued with a little more strength but a lot less time, but he didn't mind...

because there was another hole in which to fall, deeper and warmer but quiet and shouting all at once, and the music was better but the ending was visible before the start. He knew in his soul that he could crash and burn, if he let his gaze wander from the road, and looked into the wrong eyes again. For he knew that the mortal decision from so long ago was closer than ever, and wondered if the spirit of the forlorn one in his pocket would be his downfall. The sky was bluer than grey but happiness was a sin when the blue was not complete. The dolphin passed overhead, the clock ticking louder than thunder, reminding him. In his mind he could not dash her spirit to the ground, nor his it is true (for that he was yet too

weak), so he decided to continue, and listen for the confusion
he knew, and walk.

(03.09.97)

17.

too much wine can change your vision,
but it can help you see

weird. A week that went by like a flock of birds in
confused formations, nothing happening like it was supposed
to. Directions were followed that were not planned or
expected, like finding honey in a place that seemed to promise
the bitterest of potions. Each bird flew its own way, chosen by
the wind, experienced like intoxication, or maybe the purest
of destiny.

no choice, only follow; like your mortal soul was on
the line.

each bird had its own problems, trauma of a serious
kind when it was your own, everything too complicated for
analysis, thought was a hundred miles away, and the details
were overbearing, insistent, each shouting its own importance
to a mind that needed sleep but only saw blurs and heaviness,
the heralds of the next day in a new light but the same reality.

questions without answers. The birds found an altitude
for their flight to exist, but the four in the front and the one in
the middle could not fly together, too much was in the way.
Individualism. Feeling. Future. Wings that were controlled by

some other force and did not answer to the commands and went their own way, driven like locomotives that jumped the tracks and crossed the country, seeing what they wanted to see, in the colours they wanted to paint. For the birds and the trains parted the land, had the same characteristics. An incomplete, barren freedom that looked like the creations of mortal observing minds and never felt by the immortal ones who needed to feel, even though they believed not in feeling, only directions that were revealed to them when they were foolish enough to listen.

no man ever saw the truth when he looked to the horizon, only the way things were, and are, and would be, if he decided not to lie to himself, and that would make him as unreal as any who walked the planet and claimed to see. For all they were, were reflections of images and lies.

and then the bird in the middle decided the only thing that would work would be to fade out, to remove itself from what could not be dealt with and never be fixed, no matter how hard it tried. But how did you fade out when you wanted the planes to fly overhead, and the trees below to be green, and all you got were birds with no wings and trees covered in plastic leaves the colour of falseness and weakness? And you were expected to fix it all, and make it happen, and you expected that too because it was the only truth of your existence, and the wings you imagined you had trailed off into nothingness when you looked to the side to see how far they went. But if that wingspan was so extensive, why didn't the wings fly, only flop around ineffectually like fish on the beach, with the hearts of dolphins but the look of goldfish, shining without warmth and cartwheeling over the sand of half-truths and facades that were the strongest things on the face of the earth? And you didn't care if the fish died of surprise and loneliness because the truth was that you were a wingless bird and it was unfair and would never be rectified, even if you got everything and everyone you ever wanted.

because life made no sense, and if it ever did, it would scare the shit out of you, and nothing would ever be the same again, and you would sit in a corner without any light to warm your soul. But then, that's where you were now.

(05.09.97)

18.

betrayal is a form of truth

as the thunder crashed against the shore in the greatest show of anguish ever to visit the earth, the walker looked into his soul and saw that he was beginning to make the mistakes again. He thought the walk had become shorter, filled with more signs of now, and then, and the future; but instead, and worst of all, the walker realised that he had slowed.

the birds were screaming in the sky, driving the dolphins from the heavens, and the sun looked down in puzzlement on a world that drove and carried and rode all at the same time, but never really turned in any other way except this same mindless churning in the black, which looked like nothing and meant even less.

and every new vision was a vision of the past, and brought no creation to existence.

the walker thought, and thought that *all wheels must complete their circle, and what was seen will be seen again.*

so he took the wheel that turned before his mind and looked at it, turning it this way and that, but it looked the same from every angle, until he turned it upside down and suddenly it looked real, and he was filled with grief.

because that was his truth and it could not be escaped: The sense had been turned on its head and it screamed and then it wept, and he knew why. Because he was here, the walker was part of this, and was affecting the balance that all understood but him.

so he turned on his heel and went the other way, and passed the other birds as he did, the ones who had meant so much without becoming anything more than things he had given the power to betray him, and they thanked him for his inconsistency and his leaving because now they were better off. And the only words he could find for them were, *I know.*

an eagle flew overhead, crying to him to join the legions that inhabited the sky, so he asked that bird,

why, do you see something in me that makes me like what you are?

and the eagle answered, *yes, you are one of us that look upon the earth.*

it's not the same. I do not look down, said the walker.

perhaps you will give us new perspective, said the wheeling creature in the sky.

yes, said the walker, *but do you see the thing in me that makes me what I am?*

the great bird drew closer and their eyes were as one. And the eagle recoiled shrieking into the sky, away from the apparition of fear and sadness and truth.

the walker continued alone, and the tape turned over

and over in his mind, playing the same song in ever increasing volume. *I give perspective. I give perspective. I give perspective.*

and then another joined, a quieter, clearer voice. *To others, that is a sin.*

so he held his head in his hands, and tried to see the *why*, but only replayed the *what* from different angles; hot afternoon, darkening twilight, cold night. And always he knew a single day was not the problem.

the problem was the wheel that turned over his life, causing the doors to creak, then yawn, then slam. All light and sound brought to him the same realisation - he was getting stupid and slow and blind to things he did not want to see.

the truth was revealed again. He had let his guard down. Something had got in.

and so he was damned.

(08.09.97)

19.

and the arrow was so true, and the days that followed so devoid of promise, that the walker could see no road, and no shoes to carry him, and a sky the darkest shade of the worst orange, and no dolphins in any ocean of the mind; so that he stopped, and turned in confusion, and turned in anguish, and turned in fear, and held his hands aloft to the heavens in question, in inevitable mimic of the cliche that surrounded him, and could not walk.

X

20.

unrequited pt. 2 (but did you even try?)

the walker stayed in the same place for someone else's eternity, and soon the stiffness that grew like a cancer in his legs spread to his heart and his mind. He fought like a man being forced into a coffin but still it touched his soul. And he fought further, pushing vainly against tons of earth he could not see but knew were there. He ignored the logic that revealed the true paths of his journey, fighting against something he could never defeat, just claw and scratch like a mouse against a tiger, or a tiger against a bullet, or a bullet against a god: using every ounce of energy could not change the fact that he was helpless.

and the cancer was the falseness that surrounded him and it thrived, stronger than he could ever be. His only defence was the walk that was dying, the inability to move resided stubbornly in his heart and he wondered what it would take to make it leave. But all the thought in the world could not bring the answer.

time? All things change in time, and the departure would arrive in his life, if he could find the strength to wait. But he would depart alone, as the walker does, as the walker must, and he realised that this was the root of another sickness.

he had changed and not seen. He wasn't paying attention. The need to not always walk alone had been born in his soul, and it had a face, and a feeling, and a life. But this need had no link to his existence, it lived away, in another world he could not comprehend, that would not let him. It came to him from time to time, the hint of promise in a universe of untruths. But it looked past him, beyond, forlorn still, to where better things revealed themselves as more than he could ever be. For the one with the blue eyes had a need of its own, and he could not be the one: his own eyes were too empty and his heart too tired, and the darkness that enveloped him drove all good things away. And like all the others, she could not see that the darkness was not his choice.

so he sat alone and looked around him, taking stock of the walk that was stalled, impotent. He saw that one bird that meant so much but could no longer look in his eyes, and could not help wondering whether it ever really did. He saw those two birds that had fluttered around him, not meaning anything, and he felt they were no loss. And he saw the one with the forlorn, blue eyes, those eyes looking past, and could not help but understand. Then he looked out across the ocean that was the sky, and watched the waves crashing against the clouds in an anger that was the only emotion that waves could feel, and tears fell somewhere in the raindrops. The music fell to earth and it was the cacophony, that had changed from sunshine to a summer night that seemed warm and fresh but dark nonetheless. He stood at the edge of the cliff he knew so well and cried to the world, *why can no one see, that I have no control over what I am?*

the music was all he had, the walk was his only solution, but it was becoming clearer that there was another need rising again. It was the need for the destination at the end of the journey, and it did not seem to exist.

(04.11.97)

graduation is departure

and it arrived, a train on no schedule, just the ability to be there when the time came. It pulled into the station silently, like a ghost along the tracks, and all the waiting ticket holders were looking the other way, except for one. The walker climbed aboard heavily, alone, his consciousness dripping with a thousand questions, too many unknowns to work up the strength to answer to even one.

as he stepped aboard the train, he and the twilight were in slow motion; the chaos that rejoiced in his brain seemed to punish him and slow the world at the same time. As it turned at this grinding, unbearable pace it was more clearly visible, but yet never slow enough to touch. And he understood without too much bitterness that his hands might never be able to grasp any part of it with any certainty.

he nodded with acceptance as he sat down and nodded further as a fatigue that he had hitherto not allowed to surface overtook him, and he began to dream.

he saw the one with the blue eyes, those eyes that were both deeper and shallower than the ability of his comprehension; both truth and falseness, neither of which he would admit to seeing; and all this just beyond the signs that said NO at every bend in the road. And the questions flew into each other, cutting him like razor blades in a whirlwind around his being. He dared not reach out, for reaching out could only have one result, the same as it had ever done. What pained him most was his inability to resolve; this had brought the whirlwind and now he must live in it, until the strength came from to step from it, and perhaps into another.

in the dream he saw the past, and from it the futures that had organised themselves into this present, the roads that led to this place and this time. Some he had walked confidently, some foolishly, others a combination of both. Had the work been done? He could not tell, but he knew that there had been no growth, only the greater need and ability to question. It had been the longest day - a morning filled with promise, a day filled with empty chaos, a night filled with reflection. And cold.

the shoes rested, and looked at him with fear, reading his thoughts. He considered apologising for breaking his promise by letting another vehicle carry him, but since they were reading his mind, he didn't bother. He was wondering if it was time to change them, and whether it was time to accept the implications. Everything would be altered, an existence in its entirety. The walker would walk new roads, but with greater or lesser conviction? He reached down and began to untie the laces, but the train rushed past the moon, lighting his world with cold, hard light; bright and strong but a mere reflection. He decide to pause, and the shoes were relieved.

but when he awoke, a great sadness was there to greet him. He looked down at his feet, but what he sought was missing. And in his mind he rushed blindly along the length of the train but it was empty. He stood at the window and cried voicelessly out into the night, striking it, trying to drive the anguish from his mind but could not. And finally he sat down again in despair and filled his mind with a thousand more questions.

So he sat with the other one, knowing that he must give it up, for this was controlled not by him, but by some other force he might never comprehend. Still he could not let go, though all the logic in the world told him he must, and he tried to love as much as possible to make it all mean something but still could not understand the loss. The worst part was knowing that a short time was all that was left, and the grief could not be escaped, and the heart would be broken though none would see.

and he could not share this with any other being, and knew that this had never really been a choice.

the train stopped, and a bright sun filled it with a fierce daylight. The walker sighed with acceptance of a world too great for his comprehension, and reached down to untie the other shoe, to let it one day find the one that was lost, for with him it never could. The train disappeared before he could think to not step from it, and he was left barefoot among the tracks that went either to or from, but always away. He felt the cold roughness of the world greet his unprotected feet with a moment of pain and the promise of more. And he felt more tired and more alone and more real than he had since a time long erased from his memory, and he knew that the red on the stone bed that gave birth to the tracks was the truth of the walker, at least for this time that was beginning.

the movement of one foot in front of the other was as always involuntary, and he walked from empty tracks through an empty station, into a world filled with things he had not yet the ability to name, leaving a small part of his life in his blood footprints with every step.

but he walked in the sun, under a blue sky. The orange was gone and the dolphins had become clouds, motionless and benevolent.

and he wondered if he would now see the madness with his eyes, instead of his soul.

(06.12.97)

48

TWO

WILDERNESS

22.

sometimes I feel as if I'm hanging from the sky.

no, maybe that's how I always feel.

it's like I'm floating and gravity is constantly pulling me down to the earth, exactly the way it's supposed to. But I never get to the ground, because I'm tied to something else up there and I don't know what it is, and it won't let go.

so I just hang there, wishing that either gravity would give up, or this invisible rope would break, one or the other, I don't care which.

but nothing ever happens and I just swing there. I'm waiting, and I'm trying to get free, at the same time.

(25.01.98)

23.

that something that was old and wise came to him again, without announcement, and handed him a page as big as a mountain, and the words on the page could not help but be read.

'he stepped off the edge of the ordinary and watched the napalm caress the world. He looked over to where the lizards played in the sandpit of nature and saw the dinosaurs look down from the clouds and smile with regret. The sounds of life played continuously from a scratched record that had been evolved away, and he wished for something new to fall to the earth. Looking up, he saw something dropping through the sky, all fire and whining noise, headlong. The people stopped and watched for a second, craning their necks to see what it was, but their necks began to hurt so they gave up and turned back to their worlds.

'he watched the fireball dive behind the hills and heard the cry of relief as it crashed to the ground. He began to walk. All around him were the bees, travelling from horizon to horizon in beautiful winding lines that undulated in the air around the treetops, buzzing either in anger or contentment, who could tell. He was careful not to disturb the lines as he passed through them, for he was too tall, as tall as the trees, and as old.

'he smiled cordially at the aging woman who drew water from the well, the child of three generations hence strapped to her back, and she smiled with a little fear, while the word *giant* hovered, unable to hide, in her thoughts. The beads around her neck danced at the sight of him, and spoke to each other of the wind that whispered down from his eyes. He continued to walk deliberately, almost as if slowed by an unseen control. A long white plane passed swiftly overhead and he lifted a large hand in greeting but it passed too quickly and he was a little sad that his attempt at communication was not enough.

'as he left the road he apologised to the trees for the obstruction of his height, and listened to the endless song played by the guitars, washing over the land and promising something that was real. The smoke rising over the hills was his beacon and he made for it determinedly.

'a sound came to his ears, faint and broken, and he realised that it was the sound of voices, arguing. He came closer and looked down upon a meeting of everything that could speak, lives and feelings and truths, talking at each other, but could detect no information passing between them or shared, and was confused at this exchange.

'he came to a waterfall and drank thankfully, for the sun was blessed with great intensity here (as all who live here can tell you), especially for him with his bald head. He continued as the last clear waterfall turned to blood behind him, and he wondered how long he must trek before he came across the otherworldly being. He wondered what it would say to him, whether it would be afraid. But he had no answers for these questions yet.

'he climbed each hillside easily, striding through the valleys between them and watching as the clouds grew in intensity, darkening thoughtfully over the landscape.

'as he walked down into a deep valley he realised that

it was wide and round, and bare: it was a crater. The fireball had landed here.

'the world was charred and sterile in this place, and he felt fear cross his brow. In the centre was a light; he walked towards it. It was small, and lay unmoving at his feet, and hesitantly he lifted it from the ground. It moved sensually in his large palm, and began to grow and he did not fear it any longer. He looked up and saw the residents of this place peer down at him from the edge of the crater. He smiled with joy as he realised what it was he held, and was proud, for it was valuable. He called across to them, his voice breaking with emotion: *it is an idea.*

'but they were afraid, turned their backs on him, disappeared from sight. He cried as the light began to fade in his palms, weak from their departure, and for half a second the clouds parted, illuminating the tall sad figure in a barren wilderness, a single ray of the sun shining down on what could have been. The clouds closed, drops began to fall upon the giant who looked down to the light that died in his hands, and his back was bent with grief. The rain began to fall, harder and harder; a storm descended and washed away all trace of change.'

and this time the walker knew better than to look for explanation in a world that seemed to have not enough.

X

smiles threaded through the desert...

smiles threaded through the morning desert like drops of dew on a brand new spiderweb, and the people were happy. In every direction the sand burned a sterile white but perfection was broken recklessly by a dark figure on the horizon, like an ant crossing the expanse of the world. He walked into their lives in a spirit of chaos, and the music was aggressive and hurtful to all who were unfortunate enough to listen. He stepped down from the sand, his feet cracked and hot from the walk, and his eyes small and painful. No greeting welcomed him so he tried to smile at the citizens, but he was tired and in his fatigue had forgotten that his smile was ugly, and of no endearment. He tried to smile with his eyes, but the damage was done and none looked into his eyes to see the truth.

so he tried to speak to them and hoped that the softness in his voice would ease their fears and cleanse their doubt, but the words came out in a strange language and meant nothing to anyone but him. He resigned himself to the place he had made for himself, and walked on into the town, and on through the town, and on into the desert beyond, through no will of his own.

the desert burned, a vast oven that baked the spirit and roasted the mind. Delirium was no stranger here, a blissful refuge for the weak, or perhaps the strong. He was not thirsty, at least not for water, and looked into the sky to watch the colours play, and saw the dolphins again, talking to each other in voices that sounded like falling trees and rushing lava, and wondered where they would go if the sky suddenly vanished and became the violent ocean, and knew in his soul that they would drown.

a star appeared in the daylight that surrounded him but he ignored it; symbols of night and cold and loneliness were not needed here. A vampire materialised in the spaces before his every step, smiling with its teeth of thirst. But it was the walker who leaned forward and drank from the neck of forever until he was alive and lucid again, and continued on, leaving a spent figure prone in the sand, one that had been foolish enough to be in a land without sustenance and cursed with immortality. And then a vehicle that was beast and machine and spirit all at once stopped before his walking feet, and he decided that this was new, and so could do no harm.

(08.07.98)

25.

smiles threaded through the midday desert like a string of those coloured lights that swayed above you at parties and threatened to give you a headache but then you drank too much and got one anyway and forgot the other reason for the hell you were in. Self-infliction was always easier to deal with anyway.

the vehicle stopped at the enclave, virtually dripping with dust, and the creak as the door opened was abrasive enough to take the rust off every brain for a hundred metres. The eyes that greeted the walker as he stepped slowly through the market seemed to float on drunken faces that bobbed to and fro on motionless bodies, and he began to lose his balance. And then he realised that this was happening because his feet were jumbled and scared from not walking, and he felt ashamed at letting another vehicle carry him, and apologised to them.

carefully holding on to the rickety stalls that had minds of their own and tried to escape at his touch, he made his way through the sparsely populated outer walkways and into the centre of the market; the place where fires dance in every eye, snakes fly from stall to stall and the world is a burning hub of lies and toothy smiles where bargains call piranhas to a feeding frenzy.

making no eye contact with anyone, especially the strange ugly creature that passed in the mirrors thrust under his nose, he found his way to the tavern and entered. Inside, the gloom was complete, and the quiet was like an old man with no voice, soundless but thoughtful. The tavern was awake.

(06.08.98)

26.

smiles threaded through the evening desert like birthdays through the year, really only important to the heads they belonged to, and decoration for the rest of us. When he emerged from the tavern with the bottle holding firmly onto his hand and wandered to the edge of town, the sun had disappeared behind the line at the end of the world, so he turned around and fixed his eyes on the opposite line and waited for it to reappear. He ended up waiting all night, but his vigil was interesting, for the people who owned the smiles in this place came to talk to him.

first the fat, old man who owned everything in the town sat beside him, flashed him a practiced smile and asked him a thousand questions; but they were all about the world beyond the desert that he could not understand, and he owned no answers. The old man was aggrieved at this rejection, but the visitor asked gently,

- *if I had the knowledge, and if I was certain of what I knew, would I not still be there now?*

then the woman about to give birth sat beside him and asked about the future of the place he had come from, and his words made her smile in resignation:

- *I suppose it is filled with life and death and hope and despair and everything I can think of.*

then the young man with the troubled thoughts sat beside him and forced a smile, and asked about the confusion that was this place, the mind, and asked what truth was there about these days. And the visitor answered,

- *I know nothing for certain, except that the mind is filled with life and death and hope and despair and everything I can think of, and so is the world outside.*

before the dawn, when the bottle was almost empty and willing to release the hand, the young woman with the only wisdom in the desert sat beside him, smiled just a little though not at him, and asked where he had been. He answered,

- *I have been in the places beyond the desert where I have asked myself a thousand questions about the world and the future and the confusion in my mind. And I long for those who can offer answer, but find only the same questions.*

- *you will find answers, they will bring you peace,* she offered, and he looked to her with hope, but there was no mirror in those eyes that looked outwards towards a world he could not see.

- *but not here,* he smiled to no one in particular, and as he disappeared over the horizon he was like a drop of dew on a coloured light on someone else's special day, threading its way through the desert.

(10.08.98)

27.

navigating storms of consciousness

a broken wave crashed into a shore somewhere, all spent and defeated, and regretted the way it was to be. Along a beach somewhere seagulls walked, but not one lifted a wing to the sky. Their eyes were downcast but their minds were still clutter and chaos in the sky, just like their brethren crows which seem to float on thermals of insanity over the people's unwanted, laying forever in mountains of discard. Clouds somewhere above were overseeing a time of great distress, but although the wrong was complete, it was without name, or character, or comprehension. For all this *wrongness* existed in the mind of one who could not name it, only be sure that it came from him, and guided his way, and ate at his soul.

he came over the desert ridge and back into the forest (where he had existed miraculously for so long without succumbing to the madness or the fear, and which he had left for so short a time and without event). His mind's distress was not a result of the trek out there; that had turned out to be without meaning and so could have done no harm. It was true that there was no real reason for this wrongness, but it seemed real, like the way a memory or a desire forms itself into a feeling: clandestinely growing, then alarmingly revealing itself.

but this was no memory or desire, for each of those had a basis, always, even when you weren't aware of it. This was something else, something drawing from the past and the future. And he could not help but wonder if there could ever be any answers for today's unanswered questions waiting in the tomorrow or, yes, any answers to the questions not yet asked.

for this distress was not of his own construction, just like infatuation with something that offered no reason for adoration. Both were feelings which could not be navigated, or even charted; you did not know where you were until you got there, and then it was too late to say, *this is not me, or my place.*

all around him the signs had not changed since he was last here, nor the directions they pointed in, and brought to him the question: was this feeling born of something already there, and missed? But this question, nervous and saddening, could not be answered either. And he could not justify further contemplation, because he had made a vow to never go backwards, to places which held nothing for him, which never had.

perhaps this was a reason to believe that the present and the current were no more than a mistake, but then came the clear thought again - just because you have reason to believe, it does not mean that you are believing the truth. There were no answers down the road of truth, because it grew beyond your feet, and you could walk forever. And even if you chose to walk the road as he had, you could not do it without one necessary tool: detachment; a desensitisation that keeps you in the world and keeps it from destroying you.

he walked alone back into the forest, back into the life he had been away from, and it was the same, except for something new... what was it, this quickness of temper being smothered by an inability to speak, and was it really him, and was it getting worse?

so to overcome the distress he sought the truth, but did not let it overcome him, as he knew it could. And to settle on a direction through more unchartered territory, he made a decision, or at least pulled one up from the depths of his being and repeated it:

fewer questions. Believe in yourself. Right or wrong.

(17.09.98)

28.

across another desert place the weather changed, pushed and pulled by the stars, and the gods, and butterflies flapping their wings in foreign lands. The lone figure emerged from the forest again, stepping into a bright, cold sunshine in which he had found comfort. The soles of his feet, long cracked and bleeding, were beginning to heal, and the deep recess of his heart, too cracked to bleed, was beginning to heal also.

time passed, like a swollen wind that wove its way arrogantly through the world fully aware that it could never be stopped, or harmed: it would simply change and change with the days of the calendar and the calendars of the century... and beyond lay millennia.

for the first time in forever, the pendulum swung over

the centre mark, crying out in release. The problems abounded, the doubts were numerous, the questions infinite; but they were problems and doubts and questions of the mind, and thought had mutated, become something clear and simple and controllable. Above, the blue sky raged with the chaos, and the figure looked up and smiled at the entertainment. Below, the ground swelled and heaved with the earthquakes of the world's diversity, and he smiled again, enjoying this ride. Beyond, the future cried out and gestured wildly, and he smiled and waved back, a player in the game.

the threshold had been crossed, the storm of consciousness had begun to subside, and he wondered if the symbols would change. The stark contrasts of dualism began to blur, metaphor grew into reality, and he borrowed freely from the wisdom and triviality of the world, laughing at the lack of meaning that would carry him who knows where.

the dolphins swam unencumbered in the sky, the barefoot figure below them wondering if shoes were really necessary for this walk, and answering, no matter. He looked to the great black bird that eyed him with suspicion and, yes, envy. For the storm had begun to abate, if only because... surely the sky can't thunder forever.

X

29.

he walked in out of these wildernesses, dressed all in black (in the desert? is he mad?) except for a painfully white shirt, shirt and jacket flapping together, loose and ethereal. The dust had found him, travelled with him through the expanse, a passenger old and experienced in the ways of the winds that direct our lives, and make our clothes flap. The dust had seen it all.

the sepia glasses had been lost, left in place he could not go back to, and he was unprotected against the frustrated sun that whined down with every step, overwhelming, complaining, insistent.

his eyes, shrunken and hurting, were tired but clear as he entered the lone building, a large, thatched structure surrounded by desert in all directions, except upwards. There was nothing else here but a single acacia, lopsided and withered, and he wondered which one had led to the creation of the other, but they both looked as old as each other, staring at one another, the only company they would ever have.

he entered, stopping inside the door and edging to the left, and everyone knew within a second that this one was not trusting. They stared, up, down, cocked their heads in mid-survey: looking at his dark, mad clothing, his dusty jacket and dusty hair.

he waited. And waited, as they watched; him fighting the overwhelming impulse to make a sudden move just to see if they jumped out of their skins and they unable or unwilling to take a breath as if that would change the world.

(11.12.98)

he stayed there for as long as he dared, busying himself as if he was walking in circles. And all the while he watched the desert, wondering if any visitor might bring news from the world beyond the thatch and the acacia. The people from the tavern came and went. They disappeared into the horizons in every direction, their feet leaving in the sand great crooked lines of prints that would multiply and tell the tales of their movement until a dry desert storm would descend (or rise?) vengefully and wipe out all trace of their existence. Until they returned to the people's watering hole, leaving new prints, tempting the storm.

his circle walk did not grow nor shrink during his long stay, just continued as he did, without questioning and ultimately, therefore, without evolving. He was aware that he was waiting, but for what he was not sure.

for the truth to seek him out, and walk into his new world, and point at him?

or for the sky to open and the hands of gods to reach down and carry him away, or tear him limb from consciousness?

one burning noontime he stopped in the doorway of the thatch that sometimes allowed him to take shade, letting the bright world beyond burn a hole into his soul, and saw a speck with the sun behind it, slowly growing larger (so slowly! agony, waiting!), portions of dark dancing around each other in the heat until they formed themselves into the figure of a young woman, slight of build, walking in slowly, the thatch and the acacia watching intently, waiting: for she held the truth in her hand. He began to tremble, for this was something, and he could do nothing, waiting, waiting. She stopped in front of him, looked up, smiling but still not at him, and he had the time to speak. He made to do so, but she held out her hand and said:

you dropped these.

and she passed to him the sepia glasses that he had left, there, in a place she must have known did not need them, and without conversation she passed him and entered the tavern, her destination. Confusion turning to clarity, he put them on, felt the flood rushing into his brain and he remembered, the world turning a familiar colour. He turned and entered the building, but of course she was not there, and he thanked his hosts for the respite they had provided. Perhaps they wanted him to remain, for perhaps they were in need of something, but his heart had not softened to that degree. Smiling, he walked into the sunlight, the smile turning to a wince even with the glasses' protection, and he rejoined the desert (his black clothes flapping, all loose and still ethereal), the thatch and the acacia trying not to weep for his soul.

(14.12.98)

THREE

THE REALM OF THE SUN

31.

every once in a while the clouds part, whether you want them to or not, and you cannot fight the flood of bright, hot sunshine, of clarity, that comes crashing down upon you and either brings the world into focus or causes it to blur, depending on you, of course. Sometimes you wince and hide, but sometimes you turn to face it, stretching your arms out and closing your eyes and just comprehending, for a moment, the meaning of ecstasy.

these moments do not come often. It is better that they don't. I could not bear all that reality, knowing so certainly that it would just reveal the falseness beneath it. But the moment is here, and this time I choose not to ignore it. The years spent learning are gone, never to return, those years that were a farewell to one time and a beginning of another; though I cannot name these times, for that would give them an identity and infer that I understand them.

the beginning of the new time - outside of learning and on the edge of earning - is halfway through, and that real world has been touched. But I am still not able to feel that either of these times has been about living my life; rather that my life is just a silently moving thing, passing through something else.

so here I am, and make ready to grasp the here and now with a firmer hand. All around there is change in those I have known (or perhaps failed to know); but the true nature of that, I cannot say.

it is not something I see with my eyes. I continue to see through something I cannot name.

(09.04.99)

32.

what you lose, you can find again.
But the feeling of loss, you can never forget.

and a whirlwind came down and swept up what was left of his memories, which he had tried so unsuccessfully to arrange, and drew them up over his head to where he could never reach them. So this was irreplaceable loss, the definition of tragedy, but for some reason (he knew there was a reason, just as he knew that he would never name it) he did not grieve. He would make up new memories; proof, edit, condense them, and they would be true: for what you do not remember never happened and what you do remember becomes who you are, even if you get the order wrong, or if the feelings mutate.

and so he remembered: he had walked in out of the desert, his black clothes flapping (is he mad?)...he had spent time without knowing how long... the thatch and the acacia had watched him... until the figure had appeared over the horizon, slight of build and pure of soul (for a thing is pure when you do not know its transgressions)... and he had looked for something in its eyes, but it had no mirror and said to him:

- you dropped these.

and she had given him the sepia glasses, the ones he had lost or left or discarded, and he put them on... the world turning that colour... a flood to his brain... (the horizon coming into focus)... and he had left, back into the desert, walking, his black clothes flapping (all loose, and unreal?), the thatch and the acacia weeping for his soul.

(09.04.99)

33.

seduction...

the new world sat up and looked into his eyes.

he walked towards it, every step brand new and shiny like buttons that hadn't been done up yet. He had waited for the goodbye's and hello's; they had come and gone like hello's and goodbye's and the world had changed infinitely without missing a beat. Nothing would ever be the same, and of course he had no idea whether it was for better or worse.

the colours were muted and the sounds needed refreshing, and he felt a little out of sync at this (at what? But he could not answer that, so the feeling was rude and really had no place being felt). So out of sync, and a little empty, and worst of all, a little slow. He looked around as the planet turned at the same speed as he did and thought,

shouldn't this make sense now?

before him lay a neat, navigable road, short and promising, and beyond that an immense blur which he refused to look at.

all those false and glittering things that were truthfully

quite unimportant (and fleeting, he knew) were there lining the road and waiting at his feet and he was reaching down to scoop them up; the pockets were hungry, for they too crave sustenance.

but he would not look at the truth, for simply knowing truth gives you nothing. And nothing would make that better, but any gold he gathered was something more than nothing, at least. And perhaps gold would buy something that could grow into reality, despite the inner voice that sang weakly (are you thinking these false and glittering things? can you not see? *See what?* The truth! *Even the truth dies from loneliness.* You cannot do this! *I will!*)

yes, the gold would buy. For even things that are bought can be counted as real. And these are the things he would buy: speed, clarity, a future.

he stood at the edge of the cliff (yes, the cliff was here), and brutally silenced the inner song.

he screamed to the new world.

and the devil sat up and looked into his eyes.

(13.04.99)

34.

buy what you didnt know you really needed

somewhere, the forest was blue fire.

all around him the colour of calm had become chaos,

and the flames leapt around him, this way and that, but governed by no law of physics, for the world burns in ways we don't even know about yet, old ways, as old as the thoughts in your head... for surely everything you do not understand must come from infinity.

the trees were engulfed by blue around the walker (yes, he is still the walker), and hissed and wailed; anger and despair. Around the walking figure they exploded, as the chemicals that made them turned into no more than volatile mixtures of hatred and surrender. And he was laughing, listening to the guitars as they pounded ruthlessly, out of control. He thought his smile would obliterate his face, as he watched delirium jump from treetop to treetop, eating away at the sky, for the sky was orange once more, and burned with its own fierceness, a flame covering every inch above.

the sequoias were crashing to the ground, giants that had become naked of all apparel except fire, so many flames, brothers and sisters dancing wildly, the offspring of the huge sun which was both in the sky and far, far from it, so big it could not be killed.

in the burning blue the walker saw a grinning face to mirror his own, and cried to Prometheus:

- *thank you, thank you, now we no longer have to feel, for we can burn.*

and for a second he thought he saw not a smile but a wince of immeasurable grief - somewhere, far from here, the birds of war were flying again, and now were dropping fire upon the faceless, and why? Because in our primitive minds, those we care about have faces, and the ones others care about do not. And so the birds of war get to do what they do best: they were halting evolution once more. But the wince lasted only a second, and the grinning face was clear again.

he danced around the falling, exploding ogre trees, watching them writhe upon the earth, pointing like a madman. His laughter reached a pitch he had never heard before, and he thought there had to be another wide-eyed, joyous maniac in the forest but of course he was the only one.

he ran through the heat, feeling it singe his hair and warm his bones, and did no deciding. The guitars grew louder and louder, another cacophony, fascinating but too loud to last. He stopped, waited for them to rise to a crescendo: *here it comes, I am about to do it*, obliterating all sound in your head, only the sounds of chaos and destruction!

...and then he made to tie the other shoe.

(20.05.99)

35.

there was little to tell the walker if a new walk had begun or the same one continued, but the new shoes were cliche: they squeaked and hurt and felt like they wanted to be anywhere else rather than penetrated by those feet. But he was ruthless, and walked, thinking: *stretch, stretch to fit me; nothing else will.*

they would, shoes always do. Unless: they're simply the wrong size, then they will not. Or unless: they were formal shoes, the kind only worn when you were somewhere you could not evade and never really fit no matter how many years you had them. Or unless they were the biggest *unless* of them all: someone else's shoes... hasn't this become complicated.

but shoes are meant to work, so you move. Or you

would be destined to sit, and sit some more, and only feel with the parts of yourself that can stay motionless and stagnant for years, and still not die.

and shoes are not bare feet, which are beautiful and real, a symbol of something not quite of this world, too pure and calm and relaxed. Though not strong enough for every road that must be walked upon.

the walker had bled from bare feet, yes, and could not survive without the shoes, yes... But that was because he was not ready, and there was something out there in the world he could not face with his feet ugly and false, impure and chaotic, and weak. So he needed the shoes, to protect against the unknown thing, whether these shoes defied the madness or brought it.

he looked down at the new shoes that waged their quiet war against his feet and asked,

- *so is it madness?*

then he looked around the forest, furtive, embarrassed. Not by the conversation, only the words in it. For we are not to speak of madness, especially not to our shoes.

we are to stay still and live in a world where the sky floats blue above (*is that what others see, it does not burn orange for them?*), where the blue sky is free of dolphins up there... where bare feet were weak and ugly and to be covered.

we are to stay in a world where truth is unnecessary, diseased, incomprehensible.

can such a place really exist?

(10.06.99)

80

...seduced.

and before long the time came again, when the walker cursed the shoes, hating them, crying the word to which there has never been an answer and never will, no matter who came down from the heavens and destroyed you for asking it... The word was *why?*

but this time the walker was smarter, he did not stay, waiting for an answer as if simply being desperate and in pain meant you deserved one.

for prejudice makes the world go round... if one was truly objective, one could not decide what one felt more deeply, could not choose what matters.

and thinking this made him hate all the more, for the walk was supposed to end where the prejudice was dead, and once again, oh again, he was in the wrong world.

so he looked at the world, but now saw only gold. Even things that are bought are real and can be counted. What cannot be derived from freedom or love can be somewhat replaced, like a tree for a forest or a fish for an ocean. And all can be painted gold, even other people, those strange things that do not exist under the orange sky.

the walk would take him to the place where prejudice lived still, but was obliterated by the gold, the one thing stronger. And the thought of this made him want to dance - you can dance with pain and rage as much as with joy - so he threw the shoes to the wolves, and said, *you will wait, while i dance with gold, the king of all that is coming.*

and the dancing figure was bent over, a thousand worlds tied to his back, only a little more than he was used to. He heard the cacophony, the only sounds that were forever, the only way he could dance. For the cacophony came to him when the pain came, and came to him when the joy came, and he knew he could count on it. And the world was turning as he danced, all that he came to know was passing and nothing taking its place. Except gold. And he smiled as he danced for he knew something that no-one else did, or everyone else did, and maybe that was why the sky's orange was turbulent and beautiful, with the dolphins returning to swim in the heavens where they were intoxicated and carefree. The cowering wolves returned the shoes, untouched, unharmed.

smile on, walker, the way it will be is coming. And then the complications would multiply, all the hatred would grow as strong as the gods and all the dark genius would show itself.

bring it on, he thought, *nothing matters now but the secret cult of my soul.*

and the walker knew this was all wrong when his nemesis came down like a bolt of lightning from the heavens (for that is where we keep it) and landed at the walker's feet, with eyes of ice and a heart filled with resolve. The devil smiled.

and the walker knew it was wrong when he laughed in the face of evil, and said, *walk with me. Walk to what is coming.*

the devil's confusion flashed at the surface.

you are weak and pathetic and stupid, whispered the

walker, knowing he was wrong to pursue the power of gold, but with ruthless joy in his eyes.

(07.07.99)

37.

fade to black

when the hatred began to abate because the pain began to move - for true pain does not wane, just relocate like a solitary animal looking for company, alternating between the clearing and the jungle - then the walker began to think clearly once more and only feel emotion as a discontented stirring in the pit of his stomach and that place 'at the base of your spine' where perhaps the soul was kept. And he was saddened and angered by this because as the hatred abated it weakened him, and made thoughts of goodness and a future creep into his mind. But it matters not, because he had felt the truces break again, snapped like the bones of a skeleton in the jaws of a hyena, its hidden strength revealed by the sight of a rotting kill. And the truces had broken in a brand new darkness, one that had descended upon him like rain, pooling at his feet and dripping from his sodden clothes.

and as he sat in the raining darkness, unable to find the shelter of light, a memory began to surface, gradually at first, then coming in shouting leaps and agonising silences, until the picture was clear and he knew the devil had found him again. But the secret, false, dark power he had gained from the easy pursuit of gold had driven the creature away, whining in confusion, speaking no words but vowing return and revenge and triumph.

the walker lay, foetus-like in the deepening blackness, allowing its level to rise above his body, a growing smile on his face. And the delirium came, foam forming maniacally at the corners of his lips and his body trembling, first with the dark cold and then shaking with excitement, his eyes shut to keep out anything that might save him. As this cold fever overtook him, something in the dark rain that was black and pure came down and obliterated all sight: and the walker was enveloped.

(08.07.99)

38.

unrequited pt. 3

the light shone upon the walker and made him feel sick.

even the darkness in his soul and the broken truces at his feet could not keep this promise from smiling into his eyes, coyly, like a sweet wind that passes you on a lonely road but cannot be followed, no direction revealed, invisible.

when the walker arrived in the town, hard and hating, losing more with every step than he ever thought possible, he was singularly unprepared. The light came at him like the train does in the tunnel, and he had nowhere to run, and was mowed down. Every muscle had screamed flight, every impulse had been ruthlessness and self-preservation. But still he had opened his arms, as the walker does, and felt the light caress his face before it fell upon him like the wrath of a thousand self-betrayals.

but the light also shone into the walker and flowed through the walker, and washed his dark desire for gold, and he felt the weight of this metal, heavier than he had realised, somehow carried away.

for the blue in her eyes had found the salt in his soul, and both were as present as a millennium ago, when he had looked into the wrong eyes and fallen. But the forlorn one now lived in her own whirlwind, the razor blades grinning in the sun, surrounded, unable to escape her fate.

so the walker emerged from the chaos, to offer when he should have ignored, to reach out with his hands, and his blood. Their eyes met, and the word *friend* formed in a tiny corner of his soul, before he dashed its heart out on rocks long standing against a violent ocean. The word changed to *help*, as he knew it would, but her own need was revealed, to him if not to her, and it was simply freedom, and they were both worlds away from fulfilment.

and though the light was more than he could bear, it warmed his heart really, for sickness is feeling, and that interminable nausea, that sinking in the pit of your stomach, means your soul has been moved, and perhaps that can't be all bad. He smiled inwardly on the moment as he reached out one last time and thought she noticed him just for a second, even through her acquiescence to her world, and sensed her razor blades diminish in number.

he collected his blood, though he suspected she must have seen it as it fell, and he resolved to feed his starved soul, whatever the outcome, and say goodbye for once in the walk.

(20.07.99)

85

no need for need,

no need for goodbye, stop at farewell.

he broke,

the walker awash in a lonely sea;

the dreams of a thousand ages coming to him,

the words of infinite sages making dim

the light of his soul.

the eyes blue,

away;

his life, his own... hers, forfeit.

in farewell, speak not the truth - for honesty is a debt

paid not by the aloof;

and he played well this role.

for razor blades dull

only by touch:

pain too is a feeling,

and how else do we look for life?

he gives, to create his own healing -

though the seeds of emptiness are rife...

for each time he sows

and does not reap.

and the future

sows, grows, reaps as such,

perhaps now there'll be no need for need

but openness and light to see;

for the sun brings speed.

and with it he may yet find

the meaning of the deep.

(03.08.99)

40.

the walker walked, and thought about what was to come. He found himself in a great valley, green and misty and cold, and through it a river wandered, just like him: ignoring the mountains on either side, the clear horizon before and the blur behind. Above, the sky was the deep orange colour of dying leaves, that colour they seem to burn before they turn brown and disintegrate.

he wondered about what would be next, or how that time would arrive. He had felt something hinting at its existence, and even now he could sense an aura in the air around him. It was that feeling, like the truth before it entered a room filled with the false, the moment when the lies begin to break down and you know someone will have to offer something real, a selected and twisted fact to balance their inconsistencies. Just to keep the structure intact, under the fear that one truth will bring another, and another, as the first few drops are followed by the rainstorm.

he wondered what that coming thing was, or if it would be able to find him if he kept walking, but the idea to halt the walk was fleeting and quickly rejected. No, it would find him. It would surely be there when the time came, in the realm of the sun under a sky that could be nothing but orange. And he would open his arms and thank someone for it.

but there were too many empty spaces in this dream, for it could only be a dream, not even a premonition. Did he have to leave the realm of the sun for a while, to comprehend something only found in cold and darkness and rain? His sky was so orange, burning incessantly and hurting his eyes. And there was no-one to give what was coming, to him. There was no-one to thank. Not yet.

through the valley all was quiet, and incredibly still in a way he had not experienced in any other land passed on the walk. He could not think clearly, could not find the hope or the fear or even the questions. It was almost unbearable. But the valley had an end, and he would soon be through it. He thanked the river for this moment of peace, knowing it was fragile and unstable and would not last. And the river smiled back, giving the walker an idea both incredible and sublime. He waded into it, feeling the cold water swirl reassuringly around his body, over his skin like the caress of something pure and magical.

on his back he floated, arms extended, his mind aware only of his fingertips as they caressed the water in return. He looked up at the sky, watching it do nothing, himself free of thought.

slowly he moved down through the valley, and again

he betrayed his shoes and was transported by something other than himself. But he could not say what it was.

(15.08.99)

41.

the silent trek had been long, weeks without speaking, and the walker was tired. He came to the summit of a mountain, and knew he had been tested; but by what or whom, he could not say. His back ached and his legs seemed not attached to his feet, those feet down there, somewhere, a wormhole away.

the hot wind had scorched his face, throwing fear and uncertainty against his skin, but he made no sound of pain. The fatigue had reached down and found its way into his bones, but he spoke not of it, not to his bones nor to himself. He had stopped many times in the ascent, suggesting to himself that perhaps this was not the way, and abandonment was the path, like the marathon runner in the moment before he gives up on finding the finish and offers rest to the burning muscles.

but the walker did not allow himself to enjoy the release that comes with quitting, he just walked silently in that way of his, which could handle anything and yet come to terms with nothing.

thankfully, there had been no rain to undermine the spirit. The sun beat down and made the world seem too bright, the colours faded and washed out, until he remembered to wear the sepia glasses; smiling as the greens grew vivid but saddened by the weakening of the blues. He wished for a cool breeze but received only that burning wind, feeling the incline grow steeper every day, the path less winding, more dry, more stony. He did not mind, feeling his body grow lighter and yet stronger as the climb took its toll.

finally he came to the low grey cloud and the only moisture in a long time, fighting his way through it, the sky soaking his skin. He emerged from the grey and was atop the peak, looking out across an ocean of cloud that undulated with waves of white, all surf and foam. He could see no ground, not even the small piece of earth under his feet, only the cloud that covered the world as far as the eye could see.

he wondered how he must appear, a lone, dark, harsh figure upright in a sea of soft whiteness, but once again realised that no matter which way he faced, he could not see himself, and never would.

he sat down, cross-legged and found something strange and new in front of him. It was a book, without title, and somehow he knew it contained infinite pages, more than all the books he had ever read. Relieved, though not yet content, he stared out over the cloud scene before him, over what eternity must look like. He decided that he didn't like the look of endlessness, so rose and made to descend and rejoin the world, but was halted by the sound of guitars, faint but beautiful. They were throaty and gutsy and real, and found their way into his soul.

he stood there for a while, his eyes closed to shut out infinity, trying to determine where the sounds were coming from. He waited, following the notes, discovering that they came from below, under the cloud, in the real world. So he said farewell to forever and descended, the book under his arm, feeling his feet return to his legs, feeling the walk continue.

(08.11.99)

42.

dig deeper

he walked looking only at the ground, waiting for its surface to change. Suddenly he stopped, startled as that old and wise entity materialised without warning in his path, gesturing at the book the walker held, waiting for the walker to read.

'water flowed over the cracks and came to rest in the areas under his soul, under the lights that were the harbingers of a future he thought he might never reach. The water was cool and clear, cleaner than himself, and he felt a little intimidated, afraid of purity. The wasp was at his side, humming silently as it floated in the corner of his eye, watching the world in a way he longed to: dancing from side to side and seeing from every angle, but without the trauma that comes with a new perspective.

'the wasp had something to say, but irritatingly could or would not speak, even though he stopped working and stared at it, threw his hands up and gestured wildly, raised his eyebrows and mouthed comic obscenities that had lives of their own. The wasp just hovered slyly, amused, inches away from the flailing arms that it knew would never strike it, on purpose or in error. So he would give up and return to the digging, while the insect would keep watch, over what he was not sure.

'the sun flowed into the earth, melting into the hills. The world turned dusky and the digger and the wasp wandered over to the stream, the place the water looked for when it fell from the skies. It was golden in the dying light, liquid wealth pouring away into the ground. He washed in the stream as the wasp visited the rocks and grasses and flowers on the bank, growing more disinterested with each in turn.

'clean, the digger emerged, though disappointed with himself for soiling the stream with dirt not of its own making, and rejoined the dig, laying down beside his tools for the night. The wasp buzzed quietly off into the meadow, to wherever wasps go when the world darkens.

'in the morning, when the digger awoke from dreams of winged creatures warring in the skies over a world not yet overrun by men, he found the wasp floating, ever silent, at his side; contemplating the secrets of the universe or perhaps the whereabouts of the next meal. What did wasps eat? Did wasps eat? Ignoring the unwanted barrage of unimportant questions, he set about the day's digging, pausing only to drink from the stream and wave his arms in frustration at the buzzing insect who only seemed to smile inwardly at the clumsy antics of the man.

'towards sunset, the digger uncovered a strange find: the body of a wasp, bigger than that of the unwanted companion at his ear. And then another, and another, until the ground at his feet was virtually a wasp cemetery, without tombstones but no less spooky than the graveyards of his own kind. Not knowing what to do, he looked over at the expressionless wasp as it hovered beside him. And in a moment it was gone. Sad, the digger waited for the return of the wasp, but it did not return that evening, or that night, or the next day.

'the next evening, as the sun stole away for its secret rendezvous with some dark creature below the horizon, the wasp returned, humming silently, but expressing nothing. And as the digger watched, the heavens became filled with millions of buzzing creatures. Through the skies came the wasps, all perfect copies of the one that had kept him company for the past days, all expressionless and silent, only their wings making any sound, a humming chant to a humming symphony, all one note. The humming soon became a droning, like bomber planes singing, and the wasps descended.

'like a single animal they surrounded him, moving so fast he could see only a dark, violent blur. The digger did not move, watching the swirling masses rise from him and back into the heavens. After a while he noticed that the wasp corpses had disappeared, removed by a sea of insects that came from a place he did not know, moved to another place he would never see. And as the wasp hummed silently at his side, he wondered at the meaning of it all.

'as if sensing this, the insect came closer, and closer, until they were literally eye to eye, and then for a second, just a second, the digger saw the eye of the wasp move. A little to the left, a little to the right, as if floating upon a permanent tear, and he had a revelation.

'the wasp was not expressionless, the humming was not silent, the rocks and grasses and flowers were not uninteresting, the questions were not unimportant, the symphony was not one note, and most important of all, the wasps were not identical. All that he had wanted to know or could have wanted to know had been there, lives and knowledge and meaning, but he had not seen. And this was his loss.

'for the wasps had come to remove their fallen brethren from the presence of the human being who had not the ability to understand, or at least not the ability to accept what he could not incorporate into his limited vision. A story had been told to the man, in his days and his dreams, but he had not listened and could not remember, and it was lost to him, forever.

'and as another night replaced another day, the digger and the wasp parted company.'

the walker read, and reread, trying to find the story within the words, trying to see what was really written. He could not, and when he looked up to ask for the wisdom he did not possess, he was alone once again.

(14.11.99)

43.

quarter-life

after what seemed like a quarter of a century, the walker, fatigued beyond measure, sat down and looked back upon the walk. In his mind the world seemed so close, and yet further away than he had ever experienced. All of the past hurried on to him like a wind in the desert, too much to bear and yet not enough to satisfy. He was contradiction; in every step he took was dualism, in every face he put forward, paradox. There was only one truth: he was the walker, but what that meant (indeed, if there was meaning at all) he had no more clue than he had before, whenever that was. Learning from every step, he had carried on, for there is no answer other than continuation, no recourse but the course already chosen. And as he thought of these things, these dichotomies of existence, he wished for something, and it felt like the first time he had asked for anything in the walk.

he wished for innocence and simplicity, the ability to think a brand new thought and feel the joy of an epiphany, not to be caught up in this endless, debilitating cycle of some kind of learning that brought no answer. At that moment, fleeting and fragile though it was, he would have made the exchange: all the knowledge he had gathered for the chance to experience again, this time without the need to ask that next question, one question that brought the rain of questions that brought the torrent that led to the flood. But the moment passed, and he believed in the road, and the walk, and the answers that must someday be found.

at this pause, this day in the life, he sat upon the cliff and looked out upon the ocean, blue and clean and endless, and let his legs swing free over the edge. He had no words to speak, no urge to jump, no need to scream. All was silent, the guitars were put down somewhere in the world, and the surf slowed to a respectable lapping at the shore below. He removed the sepia glasses, now an extension of himself, and looked out over the sea with his own eyes, painful though they still were, and wondered about the world at the other shore. The shore he could not see, away from the realm of the sun, perhaps even too far to walk... and he started to imagine this was the coming thing, that time that might be next... But he forced that idea from his mind.

there was movement in the sky, and he looked upwards for the dolphins, but they were not there; it was something else. And the walker sat upon the edge of the cliff, drinking the world in, and watched the angels fall. Even after they were gone, he sat unmoving, staring at the place that they had been, imagining the angels before time, and those of the fall tomorrow. He felt the sun on his face speaking to him ray by ray, telling him about the world under the water, down deep where even the rays were twisted and drowned, but he did not listen, lost in thoughts of the sky, of burning wings and the sting of hot wax on the back of his neck.

but the thoughts soon died in his head as he listened to the silence and waited as it found its way into his bones. The only sound was the lapping of the water as the waves rewrote the beach, one word for every grain of sand, one grain at a time.

he heard footsteps break the tranquility, but did not turn as the other figure walked to the edge and sat, a short distance away, looking out as he did. The devil did not speak, somehow ashamed or perhaps pleased at breaking the perfect quiet with its clumsy footsteps, it just stared straight ahead over the wide bluer-than-blue ocean. The walker did not speak either, out of indifference or contempt, though they are sometimes identical. This time there was no conflict between the walker and the devil, as if one were beaten into submission, but neither knew if that was so, and it was a strange truce, out here on the cliff. And as the sun set in the seamless movement of time, the walker and the devil sat at the edge of the world where they lived, and waited for the next day to be born.

(25.11.99)

44.

- *you cannot go,* he thought he heard the devil say.

- *where?* asked the walker.

but when he turned to face his companion, he was alone at the cliff's edge. The day had not arrived; still he waited for the sun to reappear, but the night grew colder, hours passing with no movement of the stars overhead, and he knew that something was wrong.

and the quiet, impotent optimism that had a place inside him looked for the meaning, the goodness in the aberration, just as it always did.

he came to the conclusion that time had been suspended, that he had been offered a pause in the walk to ask the stars for the answers.

- *what is this?* he asked the sky overhead. *And why?*

- *always you ask why,* said the stars, speaking in unison, twinkling with knowledge they would keep to themselves, their voice male and female, child and adult all at once. *Can you not be content with what?*

- *there is no satisfaction in knowing that alone,* said the walker. *I may as well not ask at all.*

- *but all the others, they are content not to ask why, are they not?* asked the stars.

- *what others?* asked the walker.

- *indeed.*

- *well?* pressed the walker. *Why have you stopped?*

- *we have not. You have stopped. Stopped here on the cliff, where we first saw you.*

- *i am not doing this,* the walker protested. *I do not have the power.*

- *no? If it is not us, then it must be you. If it is not you, then walk. Walk from here.*

the walker thought for a second, then looked down with sadness.

- *i have lost my direction,* he said, and for the first time in the walk, he sighed.

- *then wait,* said the stars. *Wait for the way to be shown.*

- *there is no time left for waiting,* said the walker, and his voice began to break. *I don't have enough time.*

the stars were aggrieved at this. They drew closer to better see the seated figure. But his head was in his hands, his mind had left them, so they returned to their positions in the heavens and waited.

for across the ocean, the other shore he thought was within reach had vanished, become a phantom, like a new idea not acted upon in time, then discarded, surely never to be resurrected. The water was blue, like the sky was sometimes before the orange returned, glowing, triumphant.

and he knew he had missed another chance, that he had lost something again, even before knowing what it really was.

- *i am living another life,* said the walker, rising to his feet, those feet on the edge where he lived. His hands were fists at his sides, those hands he could not use for anything but fists.

- *i am living a past or a future life; I don't know which. Surely this life cannot be mine. I walk from a place I cannot understand to a place I do not know exists, surviving on faith alone and yet not enough faith to make it worthwhile. I ask nothing except the right to be true to myself, and yet it is the one thing I cannot have. I hope against hope for the chance to not walk alone, but to be not alone means to not walk, and to be not true. This world calls my name, I can hear it in the wind, but it does not recognise my face or realise that my face is not my heart. I cannot leave it, though I strain against gravity every day, waiting for its pull to ease. I try to be noble, thinking that this might hold some value, but each time i find that others are the noble, others preordained. And I long for the truth to be revealed, so that the world could see, just once. But I live in perpetual contradiction, alone in the walk, walking in the world, turning in the endless night, waiting for the day. And it all comes to ask for meaning, and there is none.*

the world and the stars were silent at this, shocked or

bemused or indifferent. The silence lasted all night, this long night that had no place in the world. The walker sat at the edge, looking down. And as the day arrived, purely out of its own willpower, the stars were relieved and retreated into the heavens where they continued to burn themselves out.

(10.12.99)

45.

she came back just for a moment, the joy that lived in the sunshine, the only one he had ever wanted to call friend (if only it had been another world, and in it he wasn't himself). And she sat with him here at the edge of the cliff. But she did not see the cliff or the ocean or the sky turning orange. And he hid his eyes from her, for he knew they would betray him, and show the hurt that she did not deserve to be burdened with. He knew she saw something, she always did, but her joy was now complete, and he felt content with this alone, perhaps the only form of contentment he would ever know. He could not speak, because he knew that he would speak the truth of his walk, and there was no place for that now. Better to not speak at all. Yes, better to not speak.

when she turned to look at the world, the quiet world here, he looked at her, knowing that in his silence he had done the right thing. He was pleased to see that she looked well, that she had blossomed, that she was happy. And the pain stabbed at his heart as it always does when he does the right thing, for to give means to remove from yourself; a glass half full here always means a glass half emptied somewhere else. But this pain he welcomed, in spite of himself.

her sojourn with him was fleeting, and he could not help thinking that this meeting was their last before the era changed and their futures came. But the joy that lived in the sunshine had no place in the walk now, had no place in the future as she'd once had no place in the past. And the present could only slide silently back, doomed to fade.

he did not watch her leave, just sat on the edge, feeling the nothingness grow beneath his swinging feet, waiting for the dolphins to emerge from the orange above and sing to him. They would sing about the chaos and the lies that he would face on the path ahead. They would sing about the colour and the cacophony that would follow him. They would sing about the walk. But the walker had not decided if he would listen.

(20.12.99)

46.

the end of time

he walked into the throng with his eyes open, and waited for the new era to fall to earth. All around him the people were as one, and yet he felt the aloneness that was his own, always stirring inside. But it did not matter, there was no loneliness here, in this madness.

all around him was joy and chaos - what he had never found and what he could not escape - the paradox of his soul. The noise encompassed him, filled him and made him whole, and the walk did not matter. The lights were flashing all around him, bringing colour into focus and driving back the darkness of this insane midnight. He revelled, dancing in the dancing crowd, acutely aware of the bodies but oblivious of the faces they belonged to, and thought this was just right. Underneath his skin, the adrenalin mixed with the endorphins, and he fed on this cocktail, as time disappeared into a vortex of heat and music and the feeling that nothing mattered but this, an eternal moment.

the music grew louder and louder, drowning out the shouting and the sounds of ecstasy, a crescendo rising to meet the stars under which they moved, the stars so old they could not understand this moment, or the reason for the madness, or the people who valued time so much because they had so little of it.

the walker felt the pumping rhythm, too fast to think about, the speed of the foetus heart before it slows in an attempt to make the moments last. He felt the beat pass from person to person, making it all a dream as he moved within the knowledge that this was real. The colours of the dream throbbed with the music, dancing in this place where the past said hello to the future, where the rules gave way to chance, and cynicism met hope.

he looked around him at the spectacle, heard the laughter, felt the ground as it turned beneath him, smelled the scent of the clean night air and tasted the celebration as it passed over his lips and tongue. His mind melded with his body, and he became another entity, one that did not care what was to be found, so long as it came from this night, this warm night that no place on earth could replicate. The entity was person and soul and consciousness all at once, connected to all senses at the same time, in the world that would remain its home.

the entity saw the smiling faces as they smiled at each other, and he smiled back, fearing nothing, expecting even less. It was the last night on earth, for tomorrow the earth would be a different place, a new planet with new wind and new water and new smiles on new faces. And that was what the entity wanted. For the antidote for the incurable is change and time, and tomorrow time would start again, and the sun would shine on a world forever altered. And the entity knew this, just as the walker had known as he walked, known that nothing lasts forever unless you experience and remember, and then it can never die. And as the insanity of the midnight gave way to the new era, crashing down upon the world with cheers and celebration, light and promise, the entity reverted to the walker that was renewed, and the walker danced on, one of many, into the night.

(05.01.2000)

FOUR

HANG

47.

the prison walk

the walker, skeletal
alone in a sinking sea
feeling only with the part of himself he cannot show
existing, never being

fall, fall,
fall into the holes you dig,
a shovel cast from every emotion
a prisoner scraping the walls
here you stay

but in your heart you know
sure as the night sky will make way for the sun
sure as the silence will make way for the shout
sure as the walker will make way
for everyone, everything

tired beyond smiles

but laughter stabs the lungs like cold winter air
millipedes walking over the skin -
it stings when they stop.

do not speak
to speak is to scream,
is to violate the sanctity of nobility
unsung sacrifice is the only purity

nylon lies come to you,
flying through the air on cotton wings;
is nothing sacred?

cry into your tomorrow
time will dull the sound;

no-one will hear.

(15.01.00)

48.

unrequited pt.4 - strumming to a close

time came to the walker at once, singing the colours

of the past, ten years of his chaos squeezed protesting into one song. Only the frustrations of the present kept the weight of the future from eating at his soul like locusts over the land: too numerous to escape, too singular to stop.

he walked in a circle of pain, the pain of the mind as it comes to realise that the mistakes have been made, too complete to undo; and the knowledge that the past is unrecoverable is the moment we lose optimism. For disillusionment is not the birth of cynicism: acceptance is. Disillusionment is a process, moments within moments, part of the whole. Acceptance is one lonely moment, final, an end. THE end.

the walker kept on, surrounded by this new failure as it grew around him. As it achieved significance, greatness. As it competed with the mistakes of the past for its place in his psyche.

the colours grew on the walls of the open cell in which he had taken refuge, thinking it would provide him with a place he'd never had: a place that was his alone. But the colours were empty now, the cacophony had left. It had been replaced by new sounds, quieter, more refined, closer to the future though further from the raw truth. Still, at least, the guitars played, strumming in the air around him.

he read the words, and felt another stab at his heart as his world was set again. Not a change, but the final acceptance of what was already, always, true. All the knowledge he had gained, his power of prediction and his long-developed ability to prepare for inevitable pain were useless to him now: the one with the blue eyes had gone, finally, into the sea yonder, the ocean that sucks in all who are not watchful and paranoid and controlled by the quest. The forlorn one had found a future, as he knew she would, and his approval of this is what affected him, for it made him think. About the walk, lonely and endless, and the joy that lived in the sunshine, gone forever, and his own truth so elusive he wondered if it was even there. He found the gladness for the one with the blue eyes in his heart, and it was real, but it brought to him the memories of his own sacrifices, his own weaknesses, and worst of all, his own errors.

and his errors he accepted, in tandem with the awareness of the time he had lost, time that he would never recover.

and he had no answers, and no clear direction to walk in, and as his mind flew at a hundred miles an hour into the depths of logic, he felt the overwhelming importance of that direction, knowing it might be the only thing that would save him. So he sat in the cell, strumming, mind whirling, trying to find an answer, needing counsel, and knowing there could be none.

(21.02.2000)

49.

unsung

when the walker looked around him at the walk, so necessary yet so uncertain, he thought about the days of his past, when the ideas had been so clear and so full of direction. He remembered his adolescence, when he had come to suspect that sacrifice was the noblest of actions, a feeling that grew into the belief that unsung heroes were the true architects of a world surely doomed to falseness and frivolity were they not to commit themselves to being eternally misunderstood and neglected. Only the walk was reality, finding the truth.

the truth is supposed to set you free, whether truth is something you hide from the world, or something the world hides from you. And he was unsure which was his truth, or which lies he had perpetuated as everyone does to make the world habitable.

the earth had begun to shift beneath him, and he did not know if he was nearing something or drifting away from it, whether the sinking feeling in his soul was a warning or a reward. His mind wandered from the philosophical questions that clutter the thoughts of the discontented. It drew towards the simplest feelings that determine direction: what makes you happy and what keeps happiness from your life.

as the unsettling feelings flowed between his head, his heart and his soul, he made his resolutions as he always did, keeping to the walk like a migrating bird over the ocean that knew somewhere deep within itself where the other hemisphere was, and when the land was approaching. This faith was stronger than any faith he saw around him, and yet it was the belief that there was nothing to believe in: the knowledge that falseness always wears the face of sincerity, or the inevitability of loneliness when faced with a need for companionship. It was an *unfaith*, and worst of all, it seemed to be his alone, the outcome of all his failures.

and as the unfaith grew in the walker, devil or no devil, he watched with quiet resignation as the rain came down day after day, at first offering hope to the desert, then bounty to the dry farmland. And then the rain refused to stop, just kept pounding down, almost in imitation of the fairy tale that the false pass around like cheese and crackers at a cocktail party, waiting for the guests to take note, speaker and listener gratified, and then return to their own lives.

the rain was unfeeling and uncaring, each drop falling silently from an oblivious sky, turning the land into a vast lake from which only drowning treetops could be seen, crying vainly for rescue from the birds above that swooped down to pluck shivering creatures to safety like raptors upon field mice. The walker looked out over the newborn lake as it swallowed up some of the land we call the world, triumphant in this battle, another day in a war lasting millennia. It made the walker feel small, small enough to ignore all this unwanted truth, and continue in the walk where he was sure he mattered.

(02.03.2000)

50.

one truth

the walker came upon a stone castle revealed by the receded floodwaters, ancient and abandoned. He climbed to the highest turret to sit and contemplate the unfaith, and its hidden pursuit of freedom. Only the past had mattered in every present, every day was an attempt to come to terms with the day before it. Could this be the path to liberation? Was he really bound by his past in ways he could not comprehend, was he truly making every effort to break free?

he was certain of only one thing, one truth that rose

from the ocean and laid itself at his feet like a blessed offering returned. He knew that he had never felt like the walk was his own.

the walk was his response to a time before, a time that was split down the middle into two equal pieces. One half forced upon him, and the other perpetuated by his own weakness. And he could not help wondering if that was really the same thing.

in that time past, he had sacrificed without understanding what he had given away. And in a moment of torment and grief he realised that it was his dream.

the dream to become what he felt deep inside himself, whatever turned the machine that was his mind right from the beginning, when he had strayed from the path that others had created, pushing to a place he did not know or seek. And for years he had been searching for the path that led to the truth, the answers to the questions, though he was hesitant to name those questions - in case he left some out and could never include them again.

and now, this thing called the unfaith. The unfaith was his, and he was the unfaith, born from he alone and mirrored in no-one. Carried by the silent optimist making the most of every broken day as they saw the rippling surface and called him cynic - knowing nothing of the true turbulence deep below he was finding ways to rise above.

and the noblest of intentions would be forever trapped beneath his ugly outward visage, the reality he could never change, of looking always like the villain or the fool. Names describe us, and our faces are named, but neither names nor faces can say who we are, labels only exist to make us easier to identify, but not to understand.

he sat watching the clouds roll away to rain on someone

else, and now he wanted the walk to be his own, willing to accept all the baggage that came with it. This was the new sacrifice: *I will accept that I am what I have been unable to avoid, this mind I have been given and this face I have endured, and this easy name of idiot and liar and cynic.*

even if the truth is buried forever.

what was coming would be harder than the time before. But he felt his heart lift a little with the knowledge that this one truth had been found, the truth of the past. Even this feeling was lined with regret, for he knew he did not have the strength to reveal that truth to anything or anyone. All his strength was needed now in the walk and of far more value here.

he had already come to know the other shore across the ocean could be not reached, and yet even now did not allow himself to believe it. The other shore... the direction that existed only because no other options did... still alive in his imagination, but still as far away from his reality as it had ever been.

(26.3.2000)

51.

conversations with the devil (five)

the walker sat upon a cliff that was the castle beneath him, his legs swinging free, dreaming of eating jelly with his fingers. He watched the wind grow turbulent around him as it attempted to bring the future here, pounded by forces that would prefer to keep it hence. As he looked out over the world he was aware that the sky had turned orange above him, and winced as the forgotten pain struck and turned familiar again, eating him from within. As he doubled over he realised he was not overwhelmed, his mind was still thinking while he felt the pain, but was not sure what this meant. The wind rose and thunder began to rumble in the distance, approaching from someone else's world. He did not feel the danger in his heart, only inside where he could not reach, like knots of stabbing knives pulsing, making him shiver with an unknown fever, here this moment and gone the next. A headache began as he unconsciously clenched his teeth, but he remembered in time and loosened his grip on himself, and it passed from him.

the cold wind around him hid the arrival. As always, his nemesis advanced with the element of surprise. The walker was silent when he looked up and noticed. Still he feared the devil.

- *aren't you going to welcome me back?*

the air reeked of greed and death, even the strong cold wind could not remove the stench.

- *you're not back,* whispered the walker, closing his eyes as if that would keep the creature from being real.

- *aren't you going to ask me where I've been?*

- *you can't be back.*

- *aren't you going to ask me if I've been having fun?*

- *i don't care.*

- *oh, yes you do. You're wondering if I've been busy, what I've seen, who I've been. You're wondering where the sins are.*

the walker shut his eyes tighter, betraying himself. The

devil laughed.

- *i've been happy, happier than I've ever been, watching you fall further from your dream into the life you vowed against.*

- *what vow?* asked the walker, unable to escape the conversation.

- *the vow never to remain where loneliness would find you. The vow that would save you from yourself. What happened to it?*

- *i lost it,* said the walker, fighting the urge to weep that threatened to overwhelm him. *I lost it when...*

- *when you thought you could beat the odds, could evade the future.*

- *when I...* stammered the walker, looking up, his voice becoming clearer despite the dizziness caused by the pain within.

- *when I sacrificed it,* he finished weakly.

- *i am the future,* said the devil. *Yours.*

and in this moment a terrible clarity overcame the blur, and the walker saw, felt, and knew the truth. His future had never been bright or open or free. His was a dark, cloying mass, ever growing and rumbling closer to him as he walked forwards to it, waiting to open its mouth and swallow him whole. And this future knew he could not stop walking.

after a long silence like a bottomless hole in the earth, words, any words, broke the stillness.

- *you're not just here for me,* the walker said to the devil.

the creature smiled.

- no, I'm here for the world you walk in, too.

then the devil slipped into a crack in the wind, and disappeared.

the walker sat watching the sky, unable to determine what had happened, what was happening, or what would happen. The thunder came closer. A raindrop fell upon his hand, warm. He looked at it with fear. It was blood red.

the walker, shivering, looked out over the world and wondered what was coming. Hearing a sound behind him as he sat in the twilight upon the castle wall, the walker turned, but too late. An arm, perhaps the arm of the absentee landlord, shot out from the dark and pushed him over the edge.

(13.05.2000)

52.

stay, shut up and deal

the rain began to fall, erratic drops here and there, loners and cliques. No longer red, but made clear and pure in its fall. The air was so much colder now, icy and pessimistic. The walker dangled from the edge of the new cliff, stones stacked upon stones keeping the base of the cliff away, hidden far below. Was it a cold, pounding sea, or a cold, murky forest, or a cold, endless desert? The walker could see only a blackness beneath him, and knew it did not matter. Death waited below, death of the soul or the heart or the blood. If he lost his grip, all that would be found was an end with no new beginning.

The stones were cold against the fingers of the single hand that held him there, his right hand, and he had not the strength to lift his left. It hung weak and traitorous at his side, clutching at the air, making useless fists. He could not pull himself up. He stared down into the darkness, mesmerised. He imagined dolphins swimming up from the depths to carry him into the orange sky. Then, as a few drops of rain found him, he imagined dragons climbing the wall to be with him, breathing fire for miles into the distance, driving away the cold, heating the world. All manner of creatures, intelligent and ignorant, ugly and beautiful, innocent and guilty, came from the cavity beneath the castle. They were playing music and screaming injustice and babbling details, but every time he blinked they were gone, and others there to take their place. The people seemed to pass in droves above him, on holiday. He listened to their banter and thought it witless. He heard the lies they told each other and thought of the truths for each one. In his heart he helped them find honesty and watched as they ignored this and went on their way, laughing. Once he lifted his head and looked at them as they stared out at the vista beyond the castle. They were all blind.

after a while he noticed that he was hanging by his left hand, and wondered how the change had been made. His right was pale and cold, fingers bruised and bleeding. The wild wind came down and played with him, caused him to sway to the time of some strange dance. He could almost hear the music. It was heinous. There were no guitars.

the devil came. The creature sat upon the wall, taking the walker's place, making the walker angry and frustrated, but determined not to be broken. The devil looked out to the horizon and spoke in a strange monologue:

- i am here you are here listen to me we are one we can see they do not can't you tell. Don't look down look at me they

won't find you you can scream it's useless. It's so cold you will freeze just like me we'll be cold together will you come? I can see you can't see they are wrong we are wronger we will be right. Every day every day every day. I am here i can be here always here with you they are not with you you are ugly and unclean and useless. You are me i am you i am the devil. I am the devil.

the devil looked down and noticed the walker dangling from the castle cliff. Shock and surprise registered in the creature before the devil vaulted from the wall and shot down past him, vanishing into the blackness below.

the walker closed his eyes and tried not to breathe.

he didn't know how long he could hold on.

(13.05.2000)

53.

hang in there

the dangling figure soon lost his sense of time and space, experiencing a strange kind of sensory deprivation out here on the new cliff. He found himself staring out into the rain as it pounded him with a million icy drops followed by a million more. The vines and weeds had grown to him, curled around his arms and legs, capturing him. He hung there without having to hold himself up, arms outstretched, sacrificial to the world of the storm.

the rain was not focused on the lone figure, not brought

by the wind to fall only on the cliff. It fell everywhere in the world of the walker, damning the innocent and threatening to bring salvation to the guilty. The walker looked out into the grey clouds that had settled like ships looking for a harbour. They were wordless now, offering no wisdom to the cliff dweller.

he struggled to free himself, panicking as the time ran out and the young grew old and content in his absence. He wanted to get back to the walk, get on with the walk, be controlled by the walk: anything was better than this frustrating immobility. But he had not the necessary requirements, he wasn't even sure what they were. So he lost control and screamed to the raining world, demanding to know the way and ranting as madmen do, as if they are entitled to the answers just because they have begun to ask the right questions. For only madmen know the right questions, or perhaps this knowledge makes sane men mad.

he twisted and writhed on the face of the end of the world, attempting to break free, but freedom is bought, just like everything else, and those who cannot afford to buy remain slaves. Especially those who stopped themselves from the dark pursuit of gold. But this slave was determined or desperate, or both. He hated again, not caring that the hole in his soul, the one that ate away at him within, had returned. It twisted and turned inside him as he did the same on the cliff, sapping his strength and attacking his resolve. He wondered if he would make it.

far below the cliff the darkness parted to reveal what looked like a boat on the water, long and white, lit like a celebration of light itself, and he realised he was looking at a cruise ship. He shouted as loud as the vines around his chest would allow, calling to the dancing figures on the deck. His communication was feeble, pitiful, and he gave up, watching the ship pass on into another holiday, and the darkness return, obscuring the ocean below.

days passed and the darkness dissipated again, but the ocean had become a desert, dark and flat, with footprints in long lines disappearing into various tomorrows, travelled by the industrious, the adventurous and the rich. The walker pulled at his bonds, trying to remove nature itself from the cliff, but they were too strong and kept him from the path for which his shoes yearned. He cried out as the darkness closed in again, and waited breathlessly for another chance.

but when the darkness parted again, all that was revealed was an expanse of blue, the deep blue, warm and rippling and inviting, calm in the storm but leading to nowhere except itself. The world under the blue was hidden from him, and he closed his eyes as tight as he could, wanting the darkness to return and hide the future.

(28.05.2000)

54.

pain is timeless

the world of the walker was a cold lonely cliff on the edge of sanity, where it felt like time had sped up when you were not watching, disappearing into the past, leaving you with no time to right the wrongs. The eyes of the eternal universe were fixed upon you and nothing would distract them.

the walker hung unconscious, head bowed, almost

beaten. The devil wreaked havoc in the world, making the storm beautiful and destructive, shoving details this way and that so that they blended into chaos and attained the texture of an inevitable tomorrow. Bleeding inside and out, but ignoring the life that ebbed away from his body, the walker shut his eyes and began to thrash around on the wall, trying to loosen the bonds of his dreams. The cold had entered through the hole in his soul, and he fought to keep the dark optimism, that had served him so well for so long, away from prying eyes. But the well-lit cynicism that comes with a decaying destiny was strong now, and true.

the strumming returned to the lone figure, but the sounds were hopelessly out of tune, and he knew that in the time to come he would have to depend on himself to keep them honest, or risk losing his only source of inspiration forever. Any other sources were still so far away, no more than paper boats upon an ocean, flimsy and threatened. He vowed, in his way of hate and desperation, to keep the strumming. The vow gave him a little comfort, and this settled in his fingertips which began to tap and tweak unconsciously, keeping the faith within the unfaith.

his weak body was stronger for his slight hope, forever on the rollercoaster of feeble and able, alternating between the peaks and troughs that made the ride almost unbearable. His legs ran the race against the vines, never winning but feeling the muscles tear, then ache, then repair; growing with every healing.

his mind saw words dashing across a page, verses growing where once only stuttering thrived, form appearing from the chaotic ramblings of some script that only he could read. Or could he? The words had the potential to be beautiful in an ugly walk, though he still wanted them to be unassuming, almost hidden. Because to believe in beauty is a dangerous thing for someone hanging on the edge of the end, fastened like a prisoner to the wall of forever, an infinity that kills all spirit and leaves you a broken puppet on the rocks, whether you fell or not.

lightning flashed and a clap of thunder aimed itself at the motionless walker, waking him from the depths. Noticing the slight change that the veiled dream world had brought, he smiled slyly to himself, then re-entered unconsciousness.

(16.07.2000)

55.

conversations with the devil (six)

the past was at the forefront again, and he second-guessed the walk as always, berating himself for sins committed and chances lost. But just when he again began to think the hole in his soul was of his own making the clouds parted and a figure danced down, bringing with it a cold and an emptiness that had a life of its own.

the devil was panting and exhilarated, floating casually in the air before the walker and grinning with a joyfulness that comes only from success.

the walker hung with eyes downcast, not really seeing the blackness below. The vines and the rocks began to warm, heated by his body as they became used to him and he to them. All around an unintelligent rain fell, steady and persistent like a man who cannot accept that he will never succeed. The drops were cold but not insistent, and he survived out here, thinking and planning until he began to wonder if his bonds were there at all; then attempting escape and realising, each time as if for the first time, that they were in fact real.

- *wonderful view, isn't it,* the devil smiled. *You seem to be enjoying your stay here. Do you appreciate that you have the best view in the world?*

for once the walker was too angry to be afraid. Incensed, a fire raged within him that knew no outlet. His emotions crowded together and pumped through him like the blood in his veins, bubbling to the surface like the foulest brew in a cauldron of eternal sacrifice. But he kept the poison down, growing within him like the cancer of immobility, a new, malevolent force that ate away at every fibre of his spirit and threatened to tear his cells from each other at his slightest movement.

- *i must confess, I am growing tired of this game.*

the devil did not say which game, the one with the walker or the one against the world.

the walker was staring at the creature, his eyes threatening to burn back into his sockets, his lips clamped together too tight to tremble. Only his fingers betrayed his fury, as they clenched and unclenched fists of clear, pure adrenalin hate.

the devil hung suspended like a puppet without strings, its eyes blazing into the walker's. Languidly the devil stretched and repositioned, mirroring the binding of the walker by the vines.

- *oh, here I am out on the cliff,* the devil mimicked, voice whining and useless. The sound of inconsequence.

- *here I am with my heart exposed. Won't you take a*

shot? Everyone else has.

the puppet began to jerk on invisible strings as invisible arrows flew into it, dancing the dance of helplessness and victimhood.

oh! the puppet cried. *Not another one? Oh! Not again?* Then the devil began to laugh, possessed, triumphant.

the walker was too enraged to speak. Blood rose and fell within his soul, heated to boiling, but unable to escape. Tears welled up in pained eyes but were kept from the world by sheer will. His heart was pounding like a thousand evil hummingbirds, threatening to explode and destroy him. But he kept it all inside and waited in agony.

bored with this silence, the devil floated closer and looked deep into the eyes of the walker, trussed up like sacrificial slaughter. The devil whispered incoherences and then, with contempt and loathing, spat into the walker's face. The walker shut his eyes and winced, but nothing touched him. When he opened them again, the devil had disappeared.

(21.08.2000)

56.

the snow fell in this world on the cliff and the walker stared out into it, astounded. The audacity of the devil was evident all around him, falling like little frosted pieces of hate and fear. Everywhere he looked a white cold was smothering the world, washing out all hope and bringing a sterility that even fire was powerless to penetrate. Each snowflake was an eye, staring into his frozen soul, making contact with the iciness that betrayed him from within. The eyes were numberless, ubiquitous and insistent.

the walker, numbed by the cold (though he knew not which cold, coming from within or from without), stared open-mouthed into the distance, as the world from across the ocean was brought hence. Each fibre of his body was taut and shivered uncontrollably, fighting. But fighting the cold was the same as fighting the vines that bound him: all in vain.

he watched as the snow deepened slowly in luxurious drifts beneath him. The surface of the world rose and rose, and soon the blanket of snow was at his feet. He shuddered as the cold touched him, unable to recoil. Still the devil's environment grew, layer upon layer of white lifelessness, purifying the world with death. His feet were covered. Then his knees, injured by eons of the walk and too damaged to ever be fixed, began to scream in agony as the cold ate its way into their core and stabbed at him like daggers. He held his tongue, refusing to cry out, dreading the rising, feathery tide. He struggled as the snow reached and covered his groin, threatening to make him impotent. Then up above his chest, sealing his heart, making it pump icy blood to the rest of him. Finally the white powder reached his face and he looked out into the world that had come to his level, bringing with it all the misery and pain it contained. A minute later the devil's blanket was pulled over his head, leaving bound every inch of his skin.

he struggled but every aching muscle was trapped. This was a grave beyond his most agonising nightmare: the one almost forgotten, where the wooden sides of the coffin pinned his limbs, where every frantic scratching brought only bleeding, broken fingers. Slowly the awful panic would rise and surface with the knowledge that the weak, flimsy box was strengthened by tons of earth, packed solid, for eternity.

and as the awful nightmare, the ultimate bad trip, began to take hold of the walker, he saw a light above him. It was weak and pale, the sun bravely trying to melt the snow that bound and gagged the walker.

his mind still worked and he knew what was happening, and he begged for the sun to stop, to retreat, to leave him here in this tomb.

but the sun continued to shine, helpful, ignorant, and the devil rejoiced. For as the sun's heat melted the snow, it turned to slush, and then to water, and the walker began to drown.

the panic rose to unbearable proportions and the walker jerked awake. He was drenched in an icy sweat, confused, and still the vines trapped him against the cliff. He was unable to remember what he had been dreaming about, and worst of all, he could not figure out if he had been dreaming about the past or the future.

(21.09.2000)

57.

the poet stabs at the air

his arms bound at his sides;
eyes flowing like lava before it dies,
falling over itself in rolling waves
down the mountainside of the prison cliff

his eyes have no smile -
slapped silly with nature looking on,
the vines hold him lovingly...
licking his skin
driving him wild

no love without binding

walk, walk into tomorrow
if you can.
yesterday was agony
today is sterile, hollowing nothingness

he tries not to look down there
to where love has arrived for the unloved
a place he walked from...
where fullness grew in the guise of emptiness.
perhaps he could not see

why could he not see

...what is it now
that he cannot see?

X

faint, almost transparent, body weak, spirit dying, hope gone, the walker looked down from the cliff that was his home, and knew in his soul the way forward. He would break free of the vines that bound him, free from what was nature, his nature, his truth. He would force another truth to be born, something that would be real for all time, and even if he forgot it one day, it would still be the truth.

he was afraid that he would be afraid. He was unsure if he would be sure. He knew it would cost him. If anything went wrong, it would cost him the walk. But even in this turmoil, he knew that he would know, when the time came. He knew what he had to do.

(28.12.00)

59.

maybe pain and suffering don't have to go together

the walker regained consciousness, his body broken and heart bleeding upon rocks he was seeing for the first time.

his vision was clearer, taking in colour and texture like never before, but a great aching rose up from the muscles around his spine into his brain. Somehow his spinal cord itself was numb, as if it wasn't even there anymore. His heart was beating like a desperate locomotive trying to make it through the tunnel in case the mountain came crashing down, laughing. The rocks were large, much larger than he, and grey. And deathly cold too, but only for a few moments, for then he began to remember.

as his heart's blood trickled down between the rocks like the world's first stream, into the water a few feet away at the shore, his memories flowed out of him too, and he retrieved a few before they were lost forever.

the fall had been chaotic and beautiful, then hellish and unreal, then accepted and something close to contentment. Pieces of it resurfaced in his mind: he had vaulted forward with the last ounce of his strength, the kind of strength that makes you move forward, not the deeper kind that makes you simply live with the pain.

he tried to recall the unclear moment between the last second of determination building in him to jump, and the first one of the panic as he fell. That moment was the most fleeting in the walk, the hardest to pin down. He was suddenly sure that he never would, nor would he ever feel it in quite the same way again.

the world rushed up at him in one huge, complete mass, then receded as the vines attempted to hold him, pliable. On and on it went, he tumbling through the air like a puppet towards the rocks and water visible before him like some kind of future, then pulled back up towards the past, momentum ever receding, left to dangle between the two in a present time he only half understood.

then the vines had released him, and he had come crashing down as he always knew he would, accepting the impact, letting his body break.

he smiled as he remembered, his lips cracking as he did so, for he had won this battle, even if the end of the war was not nearly in sight. In winning, he had left more behind than he could measure, but he had gained something that looked like that elusive animal he never truly believed he would glimpse: a chance.

the pain in his back grew, then focused, and his spine came alive again. He dragged himself upright from the rocky ground, bid farewell to the world he had walked in for so long, and stumbled into the water.

the horizon was the last thing he saw before he sank beneath the waves.

(08.05.2001)

FIVE

THE WORLD ACROSS THE OCEAN

60.

the smallest things

out of the water he rose, covered in the journey, his eyes focused on something in the future no-one else could see. He was dripping with the past still, and in his heart he felt his feet were still bare and bleeding.

they wondered about him, this one, but somehow they knew not to attempt to see into him. A woman was waiting for him at the shore, and she looked into his eyes for a fleeting moment, trying to speak of herself with her eyes, but instead she held out her hand. He placed a little piece of his soul in it and she examined it. Somehow she knew of something within him, or perhaps she knew nothing at all, so she handed it back, and he thanked her gently.

the walker looked around him. This was the world across the ocean. There were people everywhere. Everything was loud. He could not hear the wind. He looked up at the sky, feeling the coldness of this place enveloping his body, wondering where it came from.

then, without warning, the clouds parted, and the sun shone down, giving light and warmth where there had been only greyness and cold for so long. The people were surprised, and pleased, but could not realise that the walker had beheld one omen, then another.

his fingers travelled up to his chest, and touched the silver piece that hung there, had hung there for years, a symbol of the place he had left behind, perhaps forever. It was warm, having drawn in some of the waning heat of his body, what remained of the warmth of the realm of the sun. The oneness of its curves reassured him. The myth it held within it, of the creature it represented, was older than this world across the ocean, older than he could ever know. The symbol knew of the trials of the walk, of everything he had been through to finally get to this point, of all he had created and lost along the way. It knew of all the energy he had expended, even energy he never knew he had. The silver came deep from the earth, and would be his touchstone. If it knew of the trials ahead, it did not say.

the walker wished he was not so tired. Then he touched the little silver symbol again, drew in a deep breath, and walked on, towards the city.

(08.05.2001)

61.

the city was a great sprawling mass of opportunities, but the walker could name none of them. He walked aimlessly for a while, eyes darting from one oddity to the next, with the banal in between, accepting all. There was no excitement within him, no amazement, and for a few moments, sneaking in amongst the mass of moments that came rushing upon him, the walker felt cheated. Let down by his own fatigue, and by his own caution. These were the things that bound his spirit, that kept him from feeling the wonderment that he could see in the eyes and hearts of others. His own heart seemed glassy and airtight.

no matter. The walker found the city easy to navigate, and in one throbbing epiphany within all this clarity, he realised that the city was made for those who walk, who traverse the day one step at a time, one touch a day, one lesson wherever one could be learned.

but this place, oh, this place, filled to overflowing with people as if they were rats, ever moving, numberless. And it was true, for they journeyed the great city through tunnels cut obscenely into the earth which he could hear crying, bleeding. But above, they were alive, they sang and wept and were one minute enthralled and the next indifferent. For every emotion tied intrinsically to a past, there was a person, small and unique and meaningless, ever laughing or overwhelmed.

he walked through it all, looking up at the world around him in the same way as every new arrival did, and was glad for his anonymity, content that no one should know to remember, he is the walker. The cold came often here, biting and blustery, and his black coat flapped loosely around him until he acquired another, leathery, earthy, real. Armed with this, and the silver talisman that clung to his neck, he entered the great chattering mass, determined to find the path. For that was the reason he was here: to find once and for all, if that were indeed possible, the road to his salvation.

for too long had he been up there, tied, heart bleeding, so long that in the end he became bound by the very earth that he must call home. Now, for the first time, he felt some teasing form of freedom, though the call of the realm of the sun could still be heard, the whispers of necessities that he dared not heed. A force pulled him back, it would always pull him, but he was resolved to make that decision for himself. One day. He had to make good this chance, to cut his way through, to make pure this freedom.

freedom came with a price, though, as everything free must in the end, and he paid in self-doubt. The insistent feeling that all rested on one chance, this one chance to make it right, and show he was good, and say he was sorry. For that would come when he found his path, or rejoined the path he had been flung so rudely from, too far to make it back, in that time before the walk, that time erased.

for now his world was the city, with its beautiful noise. The city would teach him to live in the moment. When he drank its water, it tasted false and impure, but he did not care. That would not harm him. When he looked into the eyes of its people, they seemed confused and indecisive, but he did not care. They would not harm him either. But when he looked at the city, sprawling, overbearing and disorganised, he saw a great tumble of unwritten rules in enormous tangled clouds atop it. They swirled and meshed darkly like giant angels making love in the sky, forgetting simplicity and purpose, caught up in some complex yet mindless passion.

fear compounded the doubt in his soul, making him wonder if this world across the ocean would show him his path, or whether he would be able to walk long enough in this world to find it.

he cast such thoughts from his mind, pulled his new coat of confidence around him, and walked into the wind, through the city, looking for its centre. And his own.

(02.07.2001)

62.

dolphins return

as the walker headed through the throng, overshadowed by his fears as much as the buildings around him, searching, he heard a great nerve-shattering boom. The blood in his veins stopped cold at this, and he had to force himself to breathe, just as he forced himself to look up into the sky. Above, through the grey cold of the concrete and the smoke that the city breathed, was the clear blue sky. The clouds were gone. And hanging there, suspended from the heavens like a ghost, was a dolphin. And in its teeth it clutched a clock.

Panic coursed through the walker as he stared disbelieving at the sky, and its lone inhabitant. The dolphin was nonchalant, swimming lazily in the unfamiliar blue, tail swishing as it negotiated the unseen flow. Again, the clock chimed deeply, great cascading waves of sound swirling down upon him, immensely powerful. All the sounds of the city faded into nothingness as the walker was deafened. He searched the crowds frantically, but none could see nor hear the apparition that held his brain. The people walked, blind to him as he stood among them, holding his ears, tears threatening to break from his soul.

he looked up again, but the dolphin had moved on, out of view. Still he could hear the ticking of the clock, thundering, louder than the beating of his heart.

deaf to everything else, he clutched his coat closer and tighter, and walked, suddenly cold. All around the world moved silently, as people spoke secrets to one another that were kept from him by the ticking of the clock.

he realised that the time was running out again, and there was an edge here, an end to stand upon and look down if he could not find what he sought. His quest was all that mattered now: he had to locate the centre of the city. He had to.

but he could find no assurances anywhere to say that he would succeed.

(01.08.2001)

63.

the wind, the walker and the wall

a giant, powerful wind came down, in search of someone. It found someone as they walked, somewhere in the city, heading determinedly for something the someone could not see. It found the someone locked within the journey, coat pulled around him, eyes straight ahead, heart turbulent deep within. Ecstatic, the wind swooped down into the street, and lifted the someone off his feet.

already tired from the endless prattling of people behind him, conversing in the language of corruption, the walker felt an unseen force lift him from beneath, where he had not been watching, and carry him unceremoniously from the walk. He flew through the air, fear filling his veins, and a second later crashed heavily into the nearest wall. He heard bones break from the impact, then reeled from the pain that shot through him. But he did not cry out, just slumped silently to his knees, then toppled over and lay upon the pavement, stunned.

the wind swirled above the supine figure, looking down with interest at the broken body beneath. The someone was unmoving, laying on the cold concrete as the people passed, indifferent, speaking to themselves in a thousand different tongues. None stopped to ask the someone what was wrong, or see whether he was alive, or even to steal from his unguarded pockets. Satisfied, the wind took stock of the deathlike figure, and made to move on. Suddenly, the someone got up and walked off.

the walker felt consciousness and clarity return, and rose from the cold, hard surface. All around the walker the people moved, blind to him and each other. Their chatter seemed endless and directionless. He stood, and dusted the city's dirt from his clothing. Silent, he walked on almost mindlessly, each step becoming more and more sure as his rhythm returned. The pain that racked him dissipated casually as his broken body healed itself in seconds, guided by the mind as it rejoined the walk.

the wind watched in surprise as the someone shrugged and continued on his way, the breakages in his body and soul forgotten. It was confused at this, but knew better than to try again. This must be reported. It meant something. So the wind swooped down again but this time did not touch the walking figure, continuing on its way.

the walker felt another wind pass him fleetingly, not nearly as violent and it did not affect him. But then the walker realised that the first had not affected him either. He had been flung violently from the walk, and come crashing to a halt like so many other times, that he had simply accepted it and carried on. He had looked into the nature of the obstacle and had seen no obstacle of consequence there. And he knew within himself that he could handle anything.

this thought saddened him deeply as he walked. For if he could survive anything, then nothing mattered enough to frighten him, to hurt him, to keep him from the walk. And if he could not experience fear or hurt, then there was nothing to lose, and did that not mean that nothing really mattered at all?

(08.08.2001)

64.

deep in thought, still tormented by the question, the walker trudged through the city. He did not know where he was, did not see the ground under his feet, just walked on, adrift.

the rays of the sun shone feebly here. He remembered where he had come from, the true realm of the sun, where a warmth filled the air and the ground, and all that lived in between. This sun was a false replica, its rays passing through air which somehow remained cold, before settling upon him and irritating him, trying to burn his skin. This was a temporary facade of sunshine, a veil of light waiting to be pulled back when the dark and cold were ready to be revealed. But of course, it was the same sun shining down in both places, and he avoided thinking about what that meant.

the question resurfaced. Would this feeling continue, this hidden knowledge that nothing would slow him, no hardship was enough to stop him? Was there nothing of importance then, nothing that he would fear to lose, nothing that he would love?

the sky exploded as if it had become one great flash of lightning, and the walker fell to his knees, blinded, a searing pain shooting through his brain. He cried out and looked around as the scream inside his head vaporised to silence, to find that he had entered a new place within the city. It was a green place, with grass like a regal carpet beneath his feet, leafy shrubs standing to attention all around, and yes, even a few trees. There was no concrete here, no walls. He could hear the noises of the melee around him, muffled, and knew that this place was but small, a spot of wholeness within the inconsistencies and contradictions of the city.

a great statue stood before him, iron upon stone, a man upon a pedestal. He was an old man, with a gaunt face and short, painfully sharp beard pointing down at the walker who knelt beneath his chin. He was clad in the armour of a warrior of old, with a sword and shield at his side, a knight. It was as if he stared out into another world, a past world, unaware of the city's noise attempting to penetrate this haven. Suddenly he spoke.

- *what is the matter with you?* He was looking down upon the kneeling figure of the walker.

the walker struggled to his feet.

- *what happened?*

- *what is the matter with you, I said,* said the statue testily, his voice sounding altogether normal but his lips moving agonisingly slowly, as if trying to fight the weight of the metal in which they were cast. *Do you not know better than to think that word?*

- *what word,* asked the walker.

- *the last word you thought, when you were thinking in*

your thoughts, said the statue.

- *what?* exclaimed the walker. *The last word? what, love?*

again the world exploded above him, and as the lightning attacked the sky, his brain seemed to throb and pound painfully against the inside of his skull. Overcome, he found himself unable to stand and sank to his knees again, clutching his head with both hands.

- *don't you know better that to say that word?* boomed the knight, glaring down with great anger. *It's bad enough that you're thinking it.*

- *what - what's wrong with it?* croaked the walker, the pain receding once again.

- *it's not for you,* answered the statue. *You should know better.*

angry, the walker waved his hand in a gesture of dismissal at the knight, and staggered on, down the path before him. His frustration and anger had removed all goodness from his demeanour, and he couldn't care less about talking statues, or what he was or was not supposed to say or think.

as he walked off the old warrior continued to berate him, starting to draw his heavy sword to point it at the receding figure, offering rules and advice the walker didn't want to hear. But the old knight was so slow and his metal so heavy, that the walker knew by the time the old fool raised his sword, the walker would already be gone.

the statue far behind him, the walker continued, trying to find his way out of this place. He began to notice headstones dotting the grass both near and far, and thought this was an odd cemetery, with more grass than graves. On he went, until the generous trees and shrubs parted to reveal a large structure looming. As he neared it he saw that it was a cathedral, massive and worn, made of great stone blocks, coloured glass that glinted in the sun, and carved wood from trees dead centuries ago. This building was immense, and he felt a deathly quiet here, as he approached the doors, enormous and intricate. He looked up at the spire as he walked, his movement making the clouds above seem as if they moved too, making the cathedral seem imposing, almost forbidding. Then he noticed a figure perched high up above the doors, part of the structure. It was a seraph, carved into the stone front of the cathedral, very beautiful and quite dead. *No, not dead,* thought the walker knowingly.

- *do you speak as well?* he called harshly.

the seraph stirred from its deathlike slumber, and the walker felt a pang of guilt at his intrusion, guilt which was soon dashed out and replaced by angry bravado.

- *yes,* said the seraph simply, in a beautiful female voice, the music of a deep spring turning into a fresh fountain.

- *don't you have anything to say, then?*

- *I know you,* said the seraph, staring down with wide eyes made of stone, which blinked slowly and eerily, as maddeningly unhurried as the knight's lips. *I know who you are.*

- *well, who am I?* asked the visitor.

the seraph looked at him for long moments. Then she opened her lips and strange sounds came out.

- *what?*

again she spoke, and the walker was puzzled.

- *it is our language,* smiled the seraph. *A language so old that none exist that remember all its words. I am saying words that mean who you are.*

- what did you say? What words?

- if you could enter the cathedral, you might learn more of the words, but alas, the cathedral is closed today. Perhaps return -

- what words describe who I am? interrupted the walker rudely.

- We have much to see within, and you may even find what you are looking for.

- i said, what words? repeated the walker, growing angry.

- would you like to return?

the walker waved his hand dismissively again, and turned away.

- you don't know, he said as he made to leave.

the seraph spoke again, repeating the sounds, the old sounds she had spoken before. He turned back, and looked up at her expectantly.

- broken soul, she said.

he felt a cold pain course through him at the words, and a great emptiness in his stomach, and suddenly he felt like vomiting.

- you're wrong, he hissed. *You don't know me.* He turned and began to stomp away, his feet crunching on the pathway.

- i know what you're looking for, broken soul, called the seraph after him. *I know what you're looking for.*

the walker turned again, through no conscious will of his own. Then the stone seraph spoke again, in that language he could not comprehend, long rolling sentences, telling him with her raindrop voice and her beautiful, slow-blinking eyes. For a few moments he listened and stared, mesmerised, but then it all became too much to bear, and he turned and fled back towards the city.

those sounds echoed in his heart, as he kept running as fast as he could, afraid she would translate her words and reveal all with honesty he was not yet ready to accept.

(22.08.2001)

65.

...but he knew, and slowed, and turned back. He could not run from these truths forever, nor escape the lies either, and would have to face all, to make up his own mind. So he trudged back towards the cathedral, ready to look up at the seraph with strength in his eyes and hope in his heart, and demand that she translate her truths. But when he re-entered the clearing, his entire body went cold, for there was a sight like no other to greet him.

the cathedral was a ruin, colossal injured pieces of its walls all around him, as if it had been ripped apart by the wrath of some great beast. Stone lay like the words of the seraph's language, broken, disconnected, lost. Death was claiming the great structure, with weeds making their home between the pieces, growing unashamedly over the fallen turrets, the great windows, the carved figures. The walker stumbled through the wreckage, his eyes filled with tears of fear that he had gone mad. He searched for the seraph, hoping to see her lovely cold face under every piece of stone, under every block of the great building. But the pieces were too large, some taller than he, piled up all around him, pointing at the sky. What was left of the broken walls stood silently around him. The roof was missing completely, and the sky looked like some immense hole in the world, a big blue expanse of nothingness scooped out of the universe. He realised he was inside the cathedral now, while plants pushed up through the earth almost fluidly, like green lava, insistent.

- *so you have decided to visit our church, then?* a voice trilled. A voice like a deep spring as it turned into a fresh fountain. *I am so glad you came back.*

the walker's heart leapt, and he whirled around to find her sitting atop a jagged piece of rock, smiling to herself, indifferent.

- *i thought you were d-* the walker said to the seraph, then gave up on words that made no sense.

- *the cathedral is open now,* said the seraph, stone eyes blinking blankly, in that slow way of hers.

- *what do you mean?* asked the walker. *The cathedral is... the whole place is...*

- *yes,* the seraph reassured him. *It is how it is. Do you wish to worship? If you do, a donation or small token would be greatly appreciated...*

the seraph motioned to a small golden goblet, standing proudly in the centre of the cathedral, a drop of life in a rotting ruin.

and the walker understood in one wild moment, understood it all: the way a temple looks from outside, the truth of it from within, and the only piece of it that truly endures.

he was sick to his stomach. But the sight of the seraph, pretty and innocent, made his heart soften. In spite of himself, he tried to think of a token for the cup. Then he caught the stone seraph staring unblinkingly at the silver that hung from his neck. He clutched at it, nervous.

- *are you going to translate what you said to me,* he asked. *What you said about -*

- *about what you were seeking?* asked the figure. *Is that what you wish?*

- *yes,* said the walker. *I want to know the truth. I seek the truth.* As these words issued from his lips he felt some smallish weight lift from him, for no more than a millisecond, and suspected he had crossed a faint threshold of some kind. The seraph did not notice.

- *what a pretty talisman,* she smiled.

- *I'm sure it would be of help to the cathedral,* she continued, motioning slowly to the goblet.

- *but it's mine,* the walker said. *It's important to me.*

- *if you wish our help, we must have something from you,* she said softly.

- *isn't there something else I have that you could accept?*

- *very pretty,* the seraph, said, ignoring his comment. *Silver, yes?*

- *you cannot have it,* insisted the walker. *I need it.*

- *why?* asked the seraph. *You need the truth more.*

- *but it is my truth,* the walker said, and suddenly it became clear.

his talisman hung near to his heart, and that is why she wanted it. It was true, and part of him, and a symbol of the realm of the sun. And he knew he could not abandon one truth in order to unearth another.

this one small thing would have to serve him for now, and he would have to continue, until he found what he did know he was looking for: the centre of the city. He would have to find the rest of his truths some other way. Silently, he turned from the seraph, and made his way from the ruined church, clambering over great hulks of stone discarded by the heavens.

(10.09.2001)

66.

mad, sad world

as the walker found his way out of the green place, re-entering the city, his senses were bombarded by an immense whistling, and eerie cascade of high-pitched sound that ate its way through the air, filling his ears, his head, his entire body. He clamped his hands to his ears but this did not help, so he gave up. All around him the people were walking as if in a trance, dazed, confused. Tears streamed down their faces from eyes that were blank and held no reason. The sky was covered in the streaks of planes as they cut their way through the sky, ruling lines across the world, except - and he looked again, could this be true? - the streaks were orange. His heart sank into him like a battleship into the depths of time, and he knew someone had spoken, and said something to the world. Something terrible. Something real.

he dashed forward into the city, looking for some sign

that might explain this ceaseless painful noise that sliced into his skull like a knife, and tried to ask the people what had happened but they ignored him and disappeared as they always did into the giant rat-tunnels of the city, to be replaced by ever more people who were weeping and blank; shell-shocked. He grabbed at one, and screamed, *WHAT?!*, but was rudely pushed away and he felt a deep guilt, and self-resentment for his need to know, for his weakness.

he passed through the throng as he always did, and saw a woman's face float swiftly past him in a bubble, hand clamped to her mouth in horror, listening to the voices in her head that spoke some impossible truth. Desperate to know, the walker sprinted through the city, until he found a paintbrush hovering over the pavement, abandoned by the painter who had fled, and watched as it continued to paint its pictures, the same chilling, astounding pictures, over and over as if it could not help itself, and he saw the horror for himself.

sick, he saw it, mesmerised, as another city across another ocean, a shining new city, burned with hate and terror. Lightning struck, fire raged, the world cascaded down upon itself. And people watched. Their fear turned to sadness, then blossomed into anger. Their hearts broke with a great rumbling like an earthquake from above, then flew open like a million blood-red flowers, then shut tight like the earth ending a waterfall, all in one terrible hour. The devil appeared in every crack in their crumbling pavement, laughing, delirious, orgasm racking the creature again and again.

the walker vomited, his body not wanting to believe what his mind knew was possible, so possibly real, but the people around ignored him and he felt more alone in the walk than ever he had before. It was as if the world was ending, and he had no one to stand beside as it happened.

guilty at putting his own feelings above those of the people in the shining new city, turned primeval and mindless, covered in dust, the walker vomited again. When nothing was left inside him to return to the world, he straightened up and walked on, for the first time wishing the devil wanted to talk, so he could ask the creature what it meant to do, but of course this did not happen. Fearful, the walker continued his own search, knowing that reality was coming and he needed to find that shelter which the centre of the city would provide, or risk being lost in some new chaos when it arrived.

(19.09.2001)

67.

the centre

the walker did not stop for many hours, needing the walk to continue unbroken while he searched for the centre of the city; certain that once found it would protect him from everything... for it would protect him from tomorrow, and that was the same thing.

he watched as the city grew and shrank around him just like the hearts of its citizens, feeling apart from this, like a stranger here for the thousandth time since the walk continued in this new place. He felt that he was coming to something, but could not be sure what it would mean when he got there. He tried to recall details of the walk since he had arrived upon the shores of the world here across the ocean, but found he could not remember. He only knew that the walk was long, and much had happened... But what?

then suddenly an epiphany raged around him, as random fluttering pieces of memory suddenly formed themselves into a swirling bait ball, banding together confused in his mind, being attacked and trying to escape the predator logic that pursued them. He lunged at the ball, but only a few memories seemed to end up in his grasp.

he paused for a moment, as the cold winds grew in this world, as they did periodically, winds unaware of the realm of the sun, where the warmth was always there for all who needed it. He tried hard to remember the walk in this place, the walk since he had again drew himself out of an ocean, then found the city and entered. But no matter what he did, the time was gone, had floated away on winds that knew no warmth, that went nowhere but into the cold nothingness somewhere north of reality.

he tried to remember what he had felt, what he had thought, where he had made a choice and where he found a change, but they were gone, lost in an endless river by the side of the road, bobbing into eternity like little paper boats that were destined to sink and drown in mere inches of water.

he realised that so much had happened, that changes had been numerous, that choices had been made (although, decisions governed by necessity are hardly choices; while decisions without freedom are no choices at all) but couldn't remember what those things were.

and the walker knew that all this was nothing new, just a small insight into the walk of the past, from those first steps. He realised that this was the way it had always been, even in the realm of the sun, in the forest, in the desert. He had driven himself on as he was driven on, whipping himself like his own team of horses, taking himself from one possibility to the next, one necessity after another, one forced decision followed by more.

and he had kept his head bowed, sure in the knowledge that he was accepting the present to find a way to resist the future, that he was enduring all in an effort to fashion a chance, just one chance to make it all worthwhile. But this was not the epiphany that surged through his blood like adrenalin. Instead he saw how he had coped, how he had survived: he had lived by forgetting.

the walk was no longer flowing as the blood within him, and perhaps it had never flowed that way at all. Perhaps it had been forming itself into pieces, one thousand years here, one eternity there, one day a month, one week a year. And each of those pieces were dealt with as he fought his way through them, and was traumatised, and wiped them clean to have strength to deal with the next. He could hardly remember them at all.

and at the end, all the walk would roll soundlessly into one, and that he would forget that too. He would wake one day on the road, one foot in front of the other, and not know how he had gotten there, the clothes on his back and the shoes on his feet alien to him, chosen by someone he never knew. This thought was pure terror, because it was, as the worst fears in the world, entirely possible.

tired of rolling with the punches, exhausted in his soul so that nothing showed in his eyes, the walker moved silently, invisibly between the old buildings that towered above him, and looking ahead, saw what he was seeking... the centre of the city.

and suddenly there was a great sinking within his heart, a sadness that settled predictably within him in a place it had by now made inside him and claimed as its own, nesting.

there was the centre of the city before his eyes, large, bright, new, alive. And around it, in the form of a huge encompassing shell, was a glass-like dome. It was immense, curving and stretching itself to infinity on either side, and to infinity above. It was bigger, stronger, more powerful than anything that he had ever seen. And it was orange.

speechless, he looked around, and up, and saw the clouds radiating out from the dome which he now knew was their source. Those tangled, tumbling clouds spelling out the unwritten rules that kept those within the centre in, and those without, outside.

the breath left his aching body in one huge draught, as if one sigh was the very last breath in him. But one breath was, of course, followed by another, and another, for still he was alive in this.

he stepped closer and touched the glassy, plasticky shell, and it was cold, and hard, as he knew it would be. He rapped on it, even though he knew that this was absurd: his knocking would never be answered. There was no sound, as the glass-like material absorbed his attempt at entry.

he soon noticed that to either side of him there were people trying to get in. They were slamming themselves madly against the dome, throwing gold against it, or climbing up as far as they could before slipping comically down to where they had started, embarrassed and ashamed. He tried to say that he was not like them, that he was the walker, content to walk through the centre of the city, to learn what needed to be learned and then surely pass through the dome on the other side, but there was no-one to believe him.

he saw some of those people suddenly pass him inside the dome, slipping their remaining gold back into their pockets, or trying to rearrange the lies on their faces so that no-one would notice they had come from without, and he wondered if these were indeed the ways through. But he drove that thought from his mind: his tomorrow would look back on his today, and he was sure it was better to forget tribulations than to remember transgressions.

the walker stood outside the dome for a long, long time, peering in, its orange glow against his face, though without any real warmth, wondering if the centre of the city really held... whatever it was, he did not know yet. He walked slowly around the edge, thinking perhaps this would reveal a gate, an entrance somewhere.

he would have to walk here in this hinterland, this no-man's land, this purgatory for a long while, remaining on the outskirts and biding his time, experiencing changes, making choices, forgetting or remembering them; before he found his way in, and walked on.

(29.09.2001)

68.

in decision

the walker sat on the hard concrete, leaning against the coldness of the dome, looking out into the past through which he had come. Against his back the glass-like tomb stretched seemingly into infinity, and he dared not turn to look through it again, for he both desired and feared what was inside. Instead he stared out into the world out of which he had exploded, heeding a call on the wind, but now hearing the sound of his deepest nightmare coming true. He wanted to be back where he had started, even as he yearned to be a million miles away, part of a distant star, uncaring. Torn between these two infinite promises he sat, staring unseeing into forever.

anyone who passed him, mumbling or crying or contemptuous in their own world, would have said he seemed calm as he sat there, languid, lazily casting a long deep gaze over the earth. They could not see the dragons within his soul, snapping and hurling themselves at each other a thousand feet above his world, their eyes black and piercing, their tongues lashing out like whips through the air, their cries like howls of spite and nothing else.

one dragon was pure white, open and blank in its promise, the silver ridges on its back like the fins of the time dolphin, the ivory of its teeth like tusks from a creature long dead in the realm of the sun. The other was a deep bloodless red, fire coursing along its back like liquid desire, its talons the colour of dark wine, oblivion made real. Over and over they screamed at one another in a forgotten language, the hate spewing forth from their dead eyes as they charged at one another, blaming each other for the destruction of their species, the end of true freedom.

the walker sat, bulldozed into silence by too much time debating and reasoning within the walk, and tried to decide. The unwritten rules tangled above him had grown larger, and stronger, and he was afraid a terrible rain was coming. All above him and behind him and before him was movement and chaos, meaningless and irritating thought it was, and he wanted desperately to burrow down into the earth under the concrete, and cover himself with what was once his keenest phobia, and stay there, unfeeling, unfelt, unwanting, unwanted, content.

but he breathed still, feeling his chest move through no will of his own, and he looked into the light, and he knew he could not give up.

the time dolphin came swimming through the sky, chasing its own tail as it was bound to do, until it crashed into the orange opaqueness of the dome and vanished, buying him a few moments longer, giving him the reason, if not the strength, to wait and, perhaps, even to decide.

and then, he decided.

(23.01.2002)

SIX

LAST CHANCE

it's as if a plane has crashed in the desert, and you think of the survivor as the one who shelters bravely under broken wings. He takes care of his battered body, his injured friends, bleeds upon the sand and drinks tears to stay alive. The sun burns down upon him with infinite vengeance, hating and laughing, ruthless. But still he lives, breathes defiantly, finds water where there is none to be seen, food where none grows, hope where none exists. And you want to be like him, enduring against all odds, accepting all in one long, courageous stride, surviving. But it is not true: the one who lives on, no matter what, he is not the survivor.

the survivor is the one who walks out of the desert.

he traverses the barrenness, endures mirage after mirage, hates the sun, fears the cold, defies the wind, talks to the stars. He arrives, thin and weak, hopelessly alive. His feet are bleeding from an almost endless journey. His face is scarred by fear and weeping. His brain is a turmoil joined with the sandstorms forever. His eyes are more expressive than anyone's should be, colder than he would ever have thought possible, warmer than joy made real, deeper than love itself. His voice is bitter and gentle all at once, angry yet apologetic. His body is bruised, perhaps. His soul is broken, certainly. His spirit almost crushed, but fighting still. The survivor walks out of the desert, back into the world, outwardly ragged, inwardly triumphant.

...I am still walking.

X

ante up

he walked back into the realm of the sun, his eyes hurting a little from the bright, familiar world. He was pale and emaciated, almost another being altogether, but his eyes and voice were the same. These are things that never change.

he trudged back along the dusty road that was his entrance, and looked around. The realm of the sun was the same, just quieter, more pensive, as if even the earth itself was afraid of something, of the feet that walked upon it these days. He smelled the sweetness of the air, felt the warmth of the rays upon his skin, heard the birds call to each other, *he has come, he has returned.* No friendly face was there to greet him so he was not confused, and he sat upon the ground, feeling one with the world underneath him, and listened for the news on the wind.

the chaos of tyranny had befallen this place since the devil had come, delivering the worst fate of them all: uncertainty. All details, all facts and lies and hope and fear and greed had been smelted into one, a great pulsing molten ball of uncertainty that rolled through the realm of the sun cutting down all in its path, destroying all who could not see that this moving fate was real.

so he believed too, powerless under the weight of the ever-shifting truths that were shaping every life, from the leaf to the elephant to the time dolphin itself. He acquiesced.

and when he went to find the one that had meant so much but no longer looked into his eyes, she was climbing down into a deep, dark well from which there could be no escape and he felt the words in his throat, the words that ordered him but he should speak to her instead: *Stay. Be. Live.* But there were no sounds he could utter that would not all just translate themselves into the past and his own leaving, exposing his own selfishness at journeying to the world across the ocean. So he shed a tear and watched a tear being shed in return, and simply watched it happen.

and when he went to visit the bird with the broken wing that could never heal, he sat on the ground and watched that too, the hopelessness eating at his resolve like a cancer, making him accept like never before. He wanted to give, more than he had ever thought possible, willing to end anything just to not watch her tragedy unfold, but he was powerless to stop this too, and in his weakness could only show love.

the realm of the sun took him back without admonition, allowing him his walk, pretending to ignore his betrayal. So he walked through towards the familiar desert that lay ahead somewhere, where the blue skies were bright when the orange was on holiday. Where the water was so pure it could not help but be rare. Where the thatch and the acacia had been waiting, watching endless footsteps not knowing if some were indeed his.

and when he got there, a new face was born in that place, or perhaps a new smiling look appeared on a face he had seen before, and he was intrigued.

but then he also came to want something he'd never really had before, something he must have deserved: a new idea to walk towards in the realm of the sun. And in his mind it all made sense, or at least it promised that it would not be incomprehensible, and as he approached, he reached out to touch it. His fingers were trembling, the way an oasis looks through the desert air when it is fake, and his heart was thumping like a fish beating its life out on a sandy shore. And when he touched this idea of promise, it collapsed into itself like a cardboard box with no strength left to hold its shape. His eyes stared in disbelief at his own weakness; realising that even an eternity in the world across the ocean had not destroyed belief completely, and this could never be forgiven.

so the walker found another place in the realm of the sun, a place with colour and a few other ideas and maybe even hope. And he walked, alone as ever, through these new environs, searching for something he still could not name. But before he started that search, he sat at the table, sighed with a bottomless exhaustion, threw in his chips, and resolved once again, oh again, to play the cards he was dealt.

(28.05.2002)

71.

in the world that was the realm of the sun he walked, through time and space and emotion and perception. And with every new thought came an accompanying feeling that he had passed back into a place where there was no tomorrow, no ideal ahead which he could aim for.

he had looked ahead so many times in the past, and like the gambler before the dice are thrown, he had felt there was a chance, so much of a chance, real. And like the gambler after the dice had come to rest he had realised there had been no chance at all, just an ever-rolling cube with dots like faces upon it, some laughing, some weeping, some insane. And the betrayal in these faces transformed itself, seductively, into more chances, infinite, before his eyes.

he found himself under the sun god, wondering if that quiet being remembered (since he himself was desperate to forget) that the walker had once had dreams, and in them too were faces, and smiles, and horizons made real, and little geckos that would come to him and eat from his hand and know in their hearts that this one was good, and just, and true.

but instead of the noble, humble things of his dreams, the reality was grins and grimaces, the geckos were really just dinosaurs in the rock, and before him a wide open space with nothing to see except a weak, creeping horizon that fled at the sight of him, then inched back sneakily to peer at his ugly visage, then retreated screaming when he tried to reach out and say hello.

there was an open, chattering voice here he was eager to understand, but he feared it a great deal because it quickly felt honest, and made him realise he had nothing new to understand in this place. Somehow the ever-chattering voice, popping like popcorn, reminded him that he had always seen through the eyes of tomorrow, but now every dream had been chased. Every dragon had been caught by the tail by traitorous sweaty palms only to be released with a sigh so loud it shook his heart. And so the voice was like a record playing the past, reminding him of how the future looks: open, then closed, then twisted, then chopped up into little pieces with a knife that cuts possibilities in every way but the one you need. The voice was somehow seeping into him and edging its way through the cracks in his soul, discovering who he had been before the time was caught on the wind and taken away to a place from where nothing ever really returns.

the walker was so tired he spoke to the one with the

popcorn voice while they took thick, sweet, dark golden liquid and warmed their insides with it, and he let the truth fall from his lips in little pieces that were either gathered or discarded by the listener, for each of those actions looks the same. He ignored his own soul when it cried out in warning, anxious at feeling his guard begin to drop, and so he let the truths get out there, into the air, rolling over the ground, bumping into each other as truths do. And he let the voice tell its own truths, knowing that between the lines were more lines, and that the reality of this exchange was that the voice speaking to him would be temporary. It would soon tire of him, and become quiet or speak elsewhere. For of course it could be no other way.

as ever, the needs of tomorrow remained, insistent, like little buzzing insects that found something fascinating with his hair and would not leave him alone. He tried to listen to the needs and speak to them, appearing like the inmate who rocks back and forth ceaselessly to the rhythm of some inalterable truth, unable to escape the inevitability of padded walls.

but the needs of tomorrow knew he would not find his way into their realm, that he was walking to find the exit from today once more, even though the only way out had been blasted to rubble before him, seemingly for the last time.

so he walked, knowing there was no direction whatsoever. He had seen direction before, and known its honesty, and followed dutifully, and to his own self was true. And the knowledge of that virtue had made his failure overwhelming.

...so wet filmy things are laid over the doorways, making it harder to find your way out, and they are cold and clammy like the fingers of the lies you once told, trying desperately to hold onto you, to gain you for themselves, like cobwebs of cold, grey, syrupy saliva that will never find a way back into your mouth. Wandering the halls like an outraged soul changes nothing, and fear brings no realisation, just as logical thought generates no possible solution. Throwing yourself into whatever you find naked at your feet, mindless and monotonous and noisy, does not fill the void. Remembering all whom you cared about, whether they care in return or not, does not warm your heart, or comfort your soul, or give you hope. Trying to be noble, thinking there might be some reward coming your way in the face of another before you die someday, does not change the fact that no one cares, or ever will.

wishing you were back there, tied to a cliff, bound by something other than your own inadequacy, forces you to accept that this time you are all there is, and all there will be.

and the world will turn with you strapped to it, unable to escape.

(04.07.2002)

72.

and in the slow trudge that the walk had become, the walker was faced with a new vista, wide and unassuming and quite beautiful, and he stared out at it, trying to take at least one deep, clean breath before he moved on.

but as he breathed in the sugary, chocolatey air that coated this perfection, he noticed that the horizon had no line: that the world stretched outwards and upwards into the sky, like a great wave of earth that climbed up into the heavens. And the birds flew towards it with singular purpose, screeching with anger and desperation before they disappeared like arrows into nothingness, a motion that reminded him of... no, that being was not to be mentioned until there was no alternative.

but then the old woman who had been weeping for the old man, the old man who had found his head and left her in the lurch, came to stand beside the walker, before this spectacle. He heard the music come down from the sky, something familiar made new, like an old sound driven by new drugs, and was glad for the cacophony, glad to a degree he had thought he had lost. The warm summer night was over and the cacophony had changed again, as if it was searching for something else he had to think about, or keep an ear on.

the old woman smiled at him, toothless and pure, and he asked her what was happening to the horizon. She looked into his sepia glasses and pointed through them and said, *heh, eyes, eyes.*

but of course the walker did not want to know what this meant and tried to ignore her. It was no use, though, because she leaned forward like the human humanity he could not avoid and touched his face and repeated, *eyes, heh, eyes.*

he raised his hand to his face and removed the sepia glasses that had become part of him by now, and the vista changed before his naked vision, turning in upon itself and coming back down. He was glad it had righted itself, but was shocked to see it continue downwards, becoming a great earth waterfall that fell who knows where.

he looked at the old woman again and asked what this meant, and waited for her to laugh, *heh,* and she did. Then she searched her small pockets and drew from one of them a different pair of glasses, not sepia but transparent and shiny and new. They glinted, winking at the sun god, as she handed them to him and he thanked her, sure she was mad but trying to be polite.

he put them on and with a great roar the horizon slowly righted itself and became one endless line that divided the ground he walked on and the sky he walked under, the way it should be.

he knew that he must wear these glasses, and that he would never see a fair, honest horizon again without them. He suspected this all had something to do with time, but he could not be sure, and walked on towards the vista before him, ignoring the spluttering old hag behind him who cursed all he had ever known, demanding something back from him, as if he had some idea what that was.

(09.07.2002)

73.

in between afterlives

the walker continued slowly, the new, transparent glasses riding on his face like pilot fish waiting for some tasty morsel, of light perhaps, to fall their way. He was becoming used to them, unaware of whether they told his eyes lies or truths, only sure that the alternative was unthinkable.

the road ahead was dusty and never-ending, truly born of the realm of the sun. But he noticed a ray of light that danced before him, drawing lines upon the dead, sandy road, and this light was something alive at least. He realised that it kept him occupied with its movement in the space ahead of him as he walked, drawing his attention to the future (the next few seconds into the future, anyway) without the question of what it might become, and was glad for this game. So he followed it, hands in his pockets as he took every stride easily, and was unaware that he was unaware of anything else.

white clouds rolled over him like lost blankets trying to find their way back to bed, tired even as they moved. The realm of the sun had become huge and quiet, and he tried not to think of this as ominous, accepting the lull. The walker noticed nothing but the light in his path and the popcorn voice at his ear, popping endlessly, reassuring, even as he still knew it must be fleeting.

the sun god was giving its glow to the world, having its silent fight with the cold winds that kept the clouds from finding their way home, and he felt his bones warm slightly. He tried not to think about too much, although he half hoped that something would happen. Anything. Perhaps the popcorn voice would put a smile on his face, or the dancing ray of light would grow, or even a new face would speak something in his ear that was worth hearing. But no, that would mean he was looking too far into the future, and he knew what that would bring. He decided he would simply listen to the popcorn voice as long as it cared to talk, for it seemed real and its chatter was interesting. He would try not to ask what inspiration it held, for that was unnecessary.

and in this quiet afterwalk, between the storms of heart and soul, while the clouds chugged ceaselessly across the sky, the walker came across a lion cub, playing with the dancing ray of light and coughing contentedly. It looked into his face and their eyes met and he swore it smiled. He smiled back, as much to himself as the little king, and reached down as it rubbed its dizzyingly happy head against his ankles. He stroked the lion cub once, twice and three times before it ambled off, swatting the ray of light that zipped around on the dusty dead road that somehow now had four lives walking upon it. The walker stopped smiling of course, but the smile warmed on a little in his soul and he knew the lull was a good thing.

the popcorn voice was chattering, but it did not need to see the cub, and he did not point out the meeting. And on they went, the four of them, almost touching, not entirely aware of each other, all in the same sort of direction, and for the walker, this odd, short thing was enough.

(01.08.2002)

74.

so when a short time had passed the walker suggested to himself that the blue was coming out, and it seemed pure and clean and old, and nothing could change the fact that this thing looked real. And the walker laughed a little to the air and himself, and scratched his head, and wondered if this could be so. For the new smiling look on the old face that intrigued was still smiling, and was quiet and loud and true and secretive all at once. This meant something that had been hidden for so long the walker had forgotten how to recognise it. The wind whispered around his ears, *there is something, something, something,* and this sweet song repeated over and over until he could no longer be sure if the song was sung by the wind or the walker.

the walker travelled over the land in the smiling face's vicinity, drinking without the ache and smiling back without the fear, and the unknown was not something cold and black and dead. And it had been so long since the walker had walked the walk without considering the heavy history of the future to be fought, that he could not be sure if the present was, in fact, his.

but in these endearing questions a storm came, of course, and it searched the land. When it found the walker he was unprepared and vulnerable, and it dove into the space he should have been protecting, like the weak heel he did not know was Achilles' legacy. And he shouted with the injustice of it all, castigating himself for not realising that the most important thing was to protect the walk by protecting the chances, that when the chances were removed the walk was a lifeless, stalled vehicle that no one wanted to keep but the weak still needed.

he was powerless to keep the deep, dark clouds from positioning themselves like fat, bloated bishops and disease-racked knights into the spaces that might be his path, the only path he could see. So he watched the king and queen as they moved around oblivious, suspicious, hating the pawns for being pawns in a world that needed so many. And from his place on the board the walker watched the smiling face as it refused to reveal more that he needed, and still he smiled back.

the popcorn voice chattered in his ear as he walked, turning cold and closed for a moment for reasons that were best left unexplored in this place, and he took from it what knowledge it let slip. The cub had left, its throat torn out by life itself, and he wondered if it would heal. And if it survived that injustice, would it now be destined to forget playfulness and mature into a snarling great cat whose job it was to guard the continuity of a world filled with teeth and blood and roaring vengeance?

but even in this complex cauldron of the world,

the quietness of the smiling face intrigued, and suggested something that the walker was sure he did not deserve, and feared would not come to pass without great pain and fear and sorrow. Something worth the earth itself. Something true.

(03.09.02)

75.

inevitable

the walker lay there by the side of the sandy road, those deep green hills surrounding him in the distance, that great ocean of a sky above him, heavy and still. He was alone, and broken, and could not move. The fever had sat upon him for a week and he had refused to stop walking, so it had refused to leave. Just when he had escaped it the other shoe had come to drop upon him, as if it knew he was preoccupied with the fever, and was unguarded. It fell when he realised the smiling face was smiling at him, but most likely through him, to someone or somewhere altogether different, perhaps even the world across the ocean that he had just about forgotten.

the walker cursed himself for this oversight, as the walker does every time reality strikes, and lay there staring up into the sky that was changing from the mirage blue to a pure, vicious orange before his pain and humiliation. His arms were spread wide, flat against the ground he walked upon, his legs bent out under him like the accident victim foolish enough to be standing in front of the threat and too stupid to get the hell out of the way. And before any tears could even form in him, he was working it out, dumbly, accepting, wondering how to make sense of this thing.

the popcorn voice was chattering something, looking without seeing, and he knew he must rise if the voice was to be kept from his universe, kept from sliding down the slippery wet rocks that were the walker's present into the jagged dry rocks that were his futures. And when he saw the parachutes come floating down from heaven itself to pay homage to the popcorn voice and the sweet salty promise of the truths it told, he watched them fall like slow drops of fairness, sinking all around him, missing every slippery rock the walker could not hide. Each parachute was a gift, and the popcorn voice was indeed blessed. The walker was glad.

but this time the joy he recognised in another was not enough to give him strength, and the walker could not rise. He hated this weakness of his, and watched the popcorn voice skip forward into the green hills, oblivious, and he clamped his lips shut fiercely, his resolve absolute as always.

and the smiling face came upon him, and noticed he was different in his silence, but he could not smile this time, for he knew his smile would be ugly, and knew this was the reason for it all. For when the smiling face had smiled upon him, he had in those mad seconds forgotten he was the walker, whose stupid, ugly smile was destined to drive away all that came to examine him. And once they saw it and retreated, into their pasts or their futures, there was no reason to return. For what reason could there be?

here it was: she had smiled upon him only with pity, or arrogance, or drunkenness, or duplicity, and he, projecting the fool or liar once again, had smiled back.

(29.09.2002)

177

the waterfall was cool, and, true, and complete. So he stood under it, washing the sandy road from his clothing, giving the earth upon him back to earth beneath everything. The water flowed down from some hidden place, singing as it came down the mountain, a rhythm so pure he was filled with joy just to be allowed to hear it once again. The cacophony had been away for so long he had almost forgotten. But the pain he felt every time he tripped stupidly, awkwardly, was lessened by this purity: the sounds of the noise in his head made beautiful, filled with promise, and presented like a gift of hope to his small, weak soul.

and the water turned from cool to warm to cool again, from clear to colourful to a great pouring rainbow that bathed him in hues and tones of comfort, and he knew even if pain was there forever, he would have a few seconds here, a minute there, and for some that was the only true joy they would ever feel.

and the waterfall was his weeping too, tears he knew not how to shed any longer, and feelings he could just about see but would never experience truthfully ever again.

he let go of the dolphin he was holding by the tail, thrashing playfully and yet angrily under the alien liquid it could not understand, and it soared up into the sky where it hovered, dripping with fear and uncertainty like everyone else he had ever seen. And he smiled up, not knowing if he had wronged, the water cascading from his nose and lips like mercury now, beautifully poisonous. It fell from him into a silver pool in which he stood, dancing around his form like his only friend.

and the popcorn voice was quiet for once in his head, sad though this was, because his faltering steps had been revealed, and surely the popcorn voice knew by now, that once he left the waterfall the walker would be on the road to failure once again.

so while he stood there, letting the humiliation wash from him into the earth that held all the world's greatest transgressions, and listening to the cacophony as sweet angst and hope tumbled from it, he thought about the next step, and didn't want to leave this place. For the sun was hot and dry and dead out there right now, heavy and slow, enough to make the walker want to burrow into the sand and wait for the rain that might never come. But the rhythm of the cascading silvery water was around for a few minutes longer, he knew, and he would see this through until the end, before moving on into the walk, alone.

for the smiling face was still out there, blameless, and he knew the wan light in his ugly smile was yet to be snuffed out. He hesitated in one moment of anger, and almost left the waterfall before the cacophony was through, but in those seconds he found his patience, beating sadly, faint. He stayed and let the noise fall down around him, generous, holding back nothing. The smiling face could see much, though hear nothing, and he wondered what that meant.

the sky above was half blue and half orange for the first or the last time in the walk, and he tried to reach up and touch the straight line above him that separated the two, wondering: what would happen if he stripped it away from the heavens, and the colours were allowed to fight each other, free?

then in one moment of a perfect smile that no one would ever see, he knew the truth. The blue and the orange would find each other and dance violently between love and hate, hope and despair, truth and lies, joy and anguish. And the noise they would make would fall from the heavens, forcing the clouds down from the sky, and rain upon the earth. And the noise would be a cacophony, the cacophony, full and loud and colourful and warm, uplifting and beautiful.

so he listened to these sounds as they filled him with all the things he could feel but not deal with himself, falling from the waterfall above him, a cool wet place in the hot, cracked world, a veritable oasis in the walk.

(20.10.02)

77.

and of course that thing had to happen, for these days he was not strong enough to remain silent. The words had to be spoken. The truths were told. And he realised how stupid and blind and illogical he had been, even with the new glasses that were meant to make things clearer.

and the reality he finally learned was that the smiling face before him had not really been part of his reality at all; living only in days that had ended or those that would never come to exist.

and the heavy ache inside him that was his weakness stayed for days as he continued alone, through a world he could not see, under a sky that burned a colour he did not notice. The popcorn voice was absolutely silent. Perhaps the popcorn voice was not even there.

and in this true, honest present the walker walked, listening to sounds new and old as they fluttered down around him like ashes, as if spiteful clouds had cremated the rain, laughing as they presented burnt offerings to a world already so scorched. And in the fields around the silent, trudging figure, the land was ploughed, the seeds were planted, the crops grew and shrivelled in the vengeful drought.

the planet was turning.

the walker did not notice.

(27.11.02)

78.

and as a new sun rose upon a new world that looked so much like the old, so much like all of the walk, the walker kept to a path he did not choose, and came to a place he could not describe. And the road was empty except for a billion grains of sand that stared up at him with a billion dead eyes. And he almost missed the scrap of paper that lay, dusty, at his feet. But he knew from experience, the experience he had never wanted, that something was, as always, written.

but instead of the prose that had greeted the walker times before, there were only simple, lonely lines:

"You think you are alone because people do not see you. No. You are alone because they will never understand the thing they see."

and in this moment he finally knew he was destined - fated from within - to keep walking. Not building wings to fly. Unable to escape the fight against a future designed to consume him. And never knowing how to just give up.

and even as he crumpled the scrap of paper in his trembling fist, it turned to sand in his palm, a weary dust that sank heavily to the ground; like everything else becoming one with the endless road of the walker.

(04.01.2003)

79.

the walker was quiet for many moons. He spoke to no-one. He saw nothing. And as the world blew by in a white-hot blur that could not be touched, surrounded by air so noxious he could not breathe it in, still he walked.

the sun shone down with a power that he had hitherto never experienced, and he tried in vain to keep his focus, as if that would make this hot place bearable, as if all the inconsistencies and lies would melt into a constant truth under the glare of his mind's righteous vigil. But it was not to be; the questions he had always been plagued by just swarmed again, beautiful, stretching into the sky above the desert road like a cloud of big white moths who had lost their way in the daylight. They were questions about the beast he would never evade, the animal that he chased even as it chased him: the future.

the mileage ticked over in his soul as he walked, adding up like the record of his uncertainty and his failures, or counting any potential or talents he was not sure he ever possessed. And he listened, and questioned in return, and the debate was stronger than even the heat itself. His head was hung in perpetual contemplation, with his hands in his pockets and his eyes on the road as it slipped past beneath his feet.

so when the desert changed back into the tree-lined road, he was unaware. And when midday turned to midnight and the air became cool and sweet, he did not notice. And when he came into a quiet glade, with countless flowers and falling leaves and a gentle silence, he was oblivious. He was meant to walk on through, avoiding all that held promises and lies, ever on his journey to a place where he could be alone.

but then, up ahead, a figure appeared to cross the path before him and he slowed.

she was unforeseen, unheralded, unexpected. She was unlike anyone else he had met on the walk. This one had eyes deep and dark and gentle, with everything and nothing hidden behind them, the definition of honesty. Her voice was familiar and easy but it was that smile in her eyes that stopped him, *a smile that truly reached her eyes,* and he knew this was something brand new in the walk.

the walker felt his eyes smiling back and for the first time, it happened. The one with the smiling eyes was seeing the smile in his eyes, somehow not noticing the ugliness of his smiling face.

and then their hands touched here on the crossing between two paths, between the last world and the next, and for the first time in a long, long time, he did not have to think.

the words tumbled sure and guileless from his lips, before they danced in the night air. And somehow the one with the smiling eyes must have known he was the walker, though she could not know what that meant.

there was no past, present or future to watch him as he kissed her, without reservation, without uncertainty, without fear. Of course the moment lasted but a short time, just as every midnight quickly becomes yesterday, and the one with the smiling eyes moved on. But she promised to rejoin him from time to time on this road... and he believed.

the walker walked on, his hands in his pockets and his eyes on the road as it slipped past beneath his feet, but seeing everything he passed, hearing every sound, tasting the cool, sweet air on his lips.

(22.03.03)

~~THE END~~

THE FUTURE.

185

Thank you for reading

THE WALK
A JOURNAL

If you have a few moments, please leave a review at
The Walk by Elus Ives book listing on Amazon

To keep up to date on future publications,
visit www.elusivesauthor.com